THE END OF THE LINE

Gillian Galbraith grew up near Haddington in Scotland. For seventeen years she was an advocate specialising in medical negligence and agricultural law cases. Before qualifying she worked for a time as an agony aunt in teenagers' magazines. Since then she has been the legal correspondent for the *Scottish Farmer* and has written on legal matters for *The Times*. Her debut novel, *Blood on the Water*, the first in her Alice Rice mystery series, was published in 2007 followed by five more: *Where the Shadow Falls, The Dying of the Light, No Sorrow to Die, The Road to Hell* and *Troubled Waters*. *The Good Priest*, a Father Vincent Ross novel was published in 2014.

She lives deep in the country near Kinross with her husband and daughter plus assorted cats, dogs, hens and bees.

THE END
OF THE LINE

Gillian Galbraith

Polygon

This edition published in Great Britain in 2019 by
Polygon, an imprint of Birlinn Ltd

West Newington House
10 Newington Road
Edinburgh EH9 1QS

www.polygonbooks.co.uk

9 8 7 6 5 4 3 2 1

ISBN 978 1 84697 477 9

British Library Cataloguing-in-Publication Data
A catalogue record for this book is available on
request from the British Library

Typeset by Polygon, Edinburgh
Printed and bound by Clays Ltd, Elcograf S.p.A.

ACKNOWLEDGEMENTS

Douglas Edington
Lesmoir Edington
Robert Galbraith
Daisy Galbraith
Diana Griffiths
Dr David Sadler
Dr Harry Andrews
Tom Johnstone
Dr Mignon Ling

In memory of my father
Captain John Roderick Ross Edington

FIRST NARRATIVE
by ANTHONY SPARROW

Although I am a bookworm, I am also a burying beetle. I named my burgeoning undertakers' business in Fife (long since run by my minions) 'Sextons', after one. It's a little joke of mine, understood by few and, in all probability, appreciated only by myself. The sexton beetle (genus: Nicrophorus, previously the much more descriptive Necrophorus) is a type of carrion beetle, a burying beetle. But I go one better than my six-legged colleagues, disposing not only of the corpse, but also of his effects. 'Synergy', I believe it is called, in business circles. I 'clear' the houses of the dead. The Quality dead.

Actually, with infinite care, I sift and sieve my way through their abandoned possessions, sorting the gold from the dross. For all I know, in the grander establishments, London dealers may have already had their pick (Garwoods, for example), but, even so, I doubt any of their paid experts venture far beyond the capital.

Suffice it to say that I have in the course of my clearances acquired many splendid volumes, including a first edition of Defoe's *Moll Flanders*, admittedly in French and, *mirabile dictu,* a 1681 copy of Marvell's miscellaneous poems. As a physician *manqué* (an exam crib, carelessly secreted in an Argyll sock, ended all my hopes and aspirations in that direction), my speciality is rare medical books, my prize being Mauriceau's *Des Malades des Femmes Grosses et Accouchées* (3rd edition, 1681), all too lavishly illustrated. I will leave them all to my godchild, who, fortunately, has a strong stomach.

Less than six months ago, on the executor's instructions, I cleared a white-harled former manse in Duddingston village, Edinburgh. A gentleman's residence of substantial size, huddled in the shelter of Arthur Seat and overlooking the loch. Its owner, a bachelor like myself, had been killed; by a woman, the nearby newsagent told me, flashing an unattractive lopsided smile. 'Shopped here, he had an account . . .' the fellow added proudly. I nodded, eager to depart his strange-smelling little emporium.

'A local woman . . .'

'You don't say,' I lisped, raising an eyebrow and pushing an unruly edge of my paisley cravat under a lapel.

The dead man's name was Professor Sir Alexander Anstruther, a retired haematologist, and the newspapers were packed with the details, although I was not privy to them at the time.

As you may imagine, when fingering other people's possessions, perusing their bookcases, emptying their tallboys and manhandling their linen, a picture of the deceased invariably begins to emerge. That picture can only acquire further detail as one moves throughout their abode.

I characterise my clearing, loosely, as a type of sacrilege. All things once private, secret, hidden for a reason are suddenly revealed to me. Once or twice my finds have made me queasy (a pillow stuffed with grey, human hair), often uneasy; invariably there is something that surprises or shocks me. Commercial considerations aside, whatever I find I do not blab about it, recognising that the dead are vulnerable. The church organist tying a pale-blue bow carefully around her raunchy love letters does not expect the ribbon to be loosened by my rapacious fingers. But, I have taken no vow and there are exceptions. This Manuscript is one of them.

Anstruther's Georgian manse was large and, unfortunately for me as I had to expend my vital energies in it, as cold as the grave. Entering the icy hallway by torchlight on my first visit, I inadvertently brushed against an array of swords, naval and military, which hung from the wall, jangling them together and my nerves with them. As I tried to still the blades, I saw, framed beside them, what looked to me like an old torn dishrag, hardly visible through the condensation on its glass. Luckily, the little ivory plate on the mount stated 'Banner of Sir David Anstruther'. A family relic? The home of yet another ancestor-worshipper, I deduced, unsurprised.

You see, I do not need to advertise; work comes to me almost exclusively from the 'plum-mouthed Mafia' as I have, almost affectionately, christened them. A network of families stretching from Berwickshire to Caithness, all eschewing the local accent, invariably related to one another and quite capable of pouring out a mug of builder's tea for me while sipping their own smoky Lapsang from transparent porcelain. In their turn, a cartel of Edinburgh WS firms drafts their wills, conveyances and trust deeds, when not otherwise engaged in fighting, like rats in a bag, to snatch custom from one another.

Fortunately, I am known to be 'reliable', 'trustworthy' and, so importantly, 'cheap' by all the denizens of the bag.

Unable to locate the power switch, I continued by torchlight. With its sole inhabitant dead, the rooms I wandered through, though still furnished, seemed to echo with my footsteps. The same old, faded chintzes that hung off the windows peeked out from below the sheets covering the battered, oversized armchairs and sofas. A masculine scent (peaty whisky mixed with mothballs?) hung in the still, stale air. It was a man's house with not a cushion or valance in sight. And, I later discovered, this particular man cut his meat with a yellowing bone-handled knife, sported University silk ties and used, on a daily basis, a badger-hair shaving brush. When he entertained, depictions in oil of Sir Hamish Anstruther and his wife, by Watson Gordon and Partridge respectively, looked down on the guests in his dining room as they chased their stilton crumbs around their plates.

It did not take me long to realise that nothing in the place was new, comfortable or luxurious.

The extreme austerity of Anstruther's lifestyle reached its zenith in his upstairs bathroom, a room larger than my bedroom. A cast-iron bath, with a loofah on the rack, stood opposite a mahogany-seated lavatory. The place had no heating of any sort, no shower, and grey linoleum, part perished, covered the floor. A bar of pink carbolic sat in its saucer on top of the cistern, one corner criss-crossed with tiny murine tooth-marks.

Despite seeing that ice had formed in the pan, I had to plump myself down on the mahogany *tout suite* (IBS, if you must know); and imagine my horror when flitting the torchbeam about idly, I came upon a roll of hard Izal lavatory paper! The men who used that stuff might have turned the globe pink and kept it pink, but, personally, I believe their loyalty was misplaced. Who sells it nowadays? My allegiance has always been to the Andrex puppy.

A tour of the kitchen only reinforced my baleful impression of personal asceticism. A flagged floor, wooden Edwardian cupboards instead of units, and pans made, if you can believe it, of aluminium! Putting my hand into one of the cupboards blindly, I shrieked out loud as my fingers brushed against a mouse's skeleton in a trap. Under my touch, its translucent bones crumbled to dust. Leaning against a damp wall, and breathing deeply in and out to calm myself, I peered into the pantry; stone shelves, newspaper-covered, empty and musty. The place was lit by a single light bulb with no lampshade.

Beside the kitchen, a small study had been converted into a bedroom, presumably for use by the old fellow once he could no longer manage the steep staircase. The mean-proportioned hospital bed within looked fit for a child rather than an adult. It struck me then that only a monk, in an ostentatiously self-chastising order, could have felt at home in such an ill-lit, unadorned, poky little hole. Frankly, the presence of a hair-shirt tucked under the mattress, or perhaps a whip for self-flagellation would not have made me as much as blink. Perhaps, this minuscule fellow was some sort of penitent? Or was he simply asset-rich but income-poor like so many of my late clients? Or just plain odd?

The next door along the arctic corridor opened into his library, the largest room in the house. *Mon magnifique prix.* Every time I entered it, even in the sub-zero temperatures usually prevailing, the scent of decaying calf's skin, linen and paper within it made me almost dizzy with desire. Shelf after shelf of leatherbound beauties. Book plates decorated the front pastedowns of virtually all the volumes in it, some marking Anstruther's acquisition, some proclaiming them the property of his forebears. All depicted the Anstruther crest (a single armoured arm holding aloft a flail), the fading of the ink alone revealing which generation had added it to the collection. On one red-letter day, I unearthed, between a mound of university yearbooks and another heap of well-fingered haematological periodicals, an 1876 Culpeper's *Complete Herbal* (full Morocco, minor foxing), a very valuable tome. With no one to witness me, I inhaled deeply.

Despite such a library, I made hardly a pound on the Anstruther job. Why was this, you might well inquire? Vulgar curiosity, in truth, plus the fact that the man had been what I once yearned to be: a physician. And not just any old quack, but a real and unusually eminent one. My subsequent researches revealed that he had been the kingpin, so to speak, in charge of, monitoring and treating all the haemophiliacs in Edinburgh and the Lothians. So, once I had catalogued his collection, I spent far too long reading his work papers, poring over them, fantasising, and they were as plentiful as the stars above. Everywhere in the house, cupboards overflowed with them, drawers had become immoveable with them and carrier bags bulged, or burst, with them. It was as if there had been an explosion in a paper factory. In amongst some of the sheets of paper were what looked, on first viewing, like thousands of little yellow butterflies. Actually, Post-it notes, each with a scrawl in black ink on it.

By the back door lay a couple of clear polythene bags with blue and white police labels attached to them, returned effects following the trial, I assumed. Glorying in my privilege, I made free with them too. In one of them, I found an intriguing book.

Those of you who think my job dull, lack imagination. In saying that, I hope I do not sound embittered but, all too often, I have seen the eyes of some middle manager in life insurance, pet food or the construction industry glaze over at a drinks party or dinner as they discover my 'trade'. I may not 'touch base offline', 'punch puppies' or 'action' anything very much but, think – leather handcuffs concealed in the late Countess's Regency commode? A set of crumbling milk teeth in a matchbox or a collection of mantraps in a cellar? Our effects really do give us away, and the dead are so much less aggressive than the living; accessible, non-judgemental and, invariably, undemanding.

Everything about this man intrigued me, and he was a fellow bibliophile. More importantly, he had been murdered.

A trick cyclist would, if they got their hands on me again, peer over their half-moon glasses and murmur 'Obsession!' But, so what, I would parry. The evenings are long; I am not a knitter, have no interest in macramé or bowls or curling (God forbid). So, time well spent, I say.

As I sifted and sieved my way through the contents of the manse, I made a most exciting find; the dead man's journal. Once opened, I consumed it, and was, in turn, consumed by it. And, as I turned its pages (together with its copious insertions), an all too vivid impression of the fellow's last days began to emerge. His personality shone through; I got to know him, intimately, in his fragile state, beset by unbearable pressures. Plainly, by the time he wrote it he was well into his dotage, but, reading his words, I felt the growing menace haunting him, the dread that, day after day, was darkening his shuttered little world. Closing the journal, I felt compelled to find out more about him, about his end.

I did not have to imagine the man himself. On his sun-faded walnut writing desk, in the second, larger of the two studies, lay a slightly curled photograph of him taken outside the Palace. Apparently unaccompanied, he was exhibiting his KBE decoration for the photographer. A small, dark-haired man with large, deep-set eyes, sloping shoulders and disproportionately big hands and feet. Interestingly, his feet were flat, like mine, set at exactly ten to two. Yet another thing we had in common.

Other surfaces, including the soot-stained mantelpieces in the drawing room, dining room and upstairs bedroom all had framed photos on them, mostly black and white, but I did not find out who any of the individuals were. Family photos, I would guess. One, I now suspect, may have been of his younger sister, Isabel. A pretty girl.

Later in the clearing process, a particular letter I found by chance, stopped me in my tracks and gave me an unexpected *entrée* to one of the main protagonists in this melodrama. So, my curiosity knowing no bounds, I decided to use the opportunity that had been presented and follow up the dead man's story for myself; engage in a little research, a little gentle digging. I freely admit it, I enjoy burrowing. And as I burrowed deeper and deeper, the edges of something new and unexpected began to appear. In fact, my antennae began to vibrate uncontrollably. From then onwards, everything else in my life paled, seemed insignificant, wan, no more than a distraction.

The documents that I reproduce for you below are ordered precisely as the old man's story unravelled itself to me. The astute amongst you will notice that in including some of them, I have betrayed a trust. I make no apology. 'Dead Men Tell No Tales' as they used to say in the Westerns of my youth. Someone has to do it for them.

In undertaking this exercise, I have found myself in the unaccustomed role of editor. Prior to this publication, my professional writing and editing experience has been limited to the pages of Rare Books catalogues; factual, focussed works involving an impoverished vocabulary, copious punctuation and too many parenthetical sentences. Consequently, I feel singularly ill-equipped for the role I have thrust upon myself. However, my interventions have been slight, amounting to little more than the sprinkling of a few commas and full-stops and, for clarity's sake, the adoption of a more conventional use of the paragraph.

By now, you may be wondering where, precisely, I found the Professor's journal. It was secreted in the concealed drawer of a small George III cabinet by his bed. As an ancient, red cough jujube had deliquesced over it and the base of the drawer containing it, I know the police cannot have had access to it. The text of the journal was in his handwriting, the insertions were in the form of printed material that had been stapled to the lined pages. I reproduce them all below in typed form. Like our dear departed, I am an old technophobe, but in the 1980s I did forsake my Parker for a spanking new electric Olivetti.

Anthony Sparrow

JOURNAL *of* PROFESSOR
ALEXANDER ANSTRUTHER

14th February 2014

Henceforward, you must be my memory.

The one that once served me so well is, in my ninetieth year, beginning to forsake me. Dysfunctional, no longer retaining my shopping list, though, gratifyingly, holding onto the more risqué of my old med school mnemonics including 'Two Zulus Buggered My Cat' (the branches of the facial nerve). That reminds me, I must get my Rubenesque carer, Irma, to buy:

- Strawberry Jam and Peanut butter
- Electric razor
- Green bananas
- Tena pants
- Polo mints
- 2 light bulbs

I have begun this *aide memoire* because a date for the Goodhart Inquiry into the 'Tainted Blood' scandal, as the press will insist on calling it in their banner headlines, has, finally, been fixed (18th April 2014). Who is this Lord Goodhart? Self-righteous editorials assure me that their readers 'demand' to know how the public blood supply became contaminated by the HIV/AIDS virus. Do they, indeed? Judging by the Inquiry's remit, the victim groups including, doubtless, my torturers, the 'BAD BLOOD BRIGADE' must have been dancing in the street. The Terms of Reference are vast, quite vast, stretching back into the mists of history.

I have not yet been summoned but, sure as eggs is eggs, I will be. There can be no show without Punch. Fear, and prudence, dictate that I MUST consult with the three other Profs and Ken Peat. Gavin Threadneedle too, if he's still with us. All of us who treated those poor haemophiliacs who died from AIDS will find ourselves revolving on the same spit. I must also look out my records, my files from the Royal Hospital etc. from 1970 onwards; enumerate, tabulate, catalogue and re-file in chronological order.

My life will not be my own.

It does not really matter but, nonetheless, I feel I must record that today, my sweet dog died. For over a year, neither she, nor I, have been able to go for walks, but I loved whispering into her soft, silky ears and felt I had someone who listened to me, understood me. Loved me, actually. I will have no more dogs. You, journal, will be my sole confidante. I will talk to you and, like Lucky, you will not answer back. Yet again, Darling Irma forgot to water my plants.

BP 152/90

16th February 2014
Today I saw the first of the Profs, Jimmy Ward. Or, more

accurately, the bits of him that are left. I greeted him cheerily, saying, 'You look like death warmed up, old man!'. He stared at me, equally aghast, his marked *arcus senilis* having made his brown eyes blue (as the lovely Crystal Gayle used to sing), and then led me inside the furniture storeroom that passes for his home. To think for the entire twenty-five years that I was Prof of Haematology Medicine in Edinburgh he remained in charge in Glasgow, despite his notoriously short fuse. Margery was slumped, slack-jawed, in an armchair, apparently asleep, so we went to his 'den'. Notwithstanding their antiquated central heating system, it was fearfully hot, but he insisted that the blow heater should remain on. We discussed the following:

1. The problem of large blood donor pools
2. Blood donor selection in the '80s
3. Haemophilia therapy in the '80s
4. The history of HIV/AIDS in our areas
5. The problem that is Dr Kenneth Peat

I have undertaken to go through my entire archive and find all papers within my possession relevant to topics 1–4. Jimmy is to do the same. He and I agreed that our Achilles heel will probably be Ken. His manners remain impeccable but, when in doubt, he takes the easy course and agrees to anything and everything. Maybe he is, indeed, 'none the wiser' as he constantly asserts? Under aggressive cross-examination he might, to use non-technical parlance, throw us all to the wolves. Jimmy looked fearful simply at the mention of his name. Then, sucking in his teeth, he said, 'And there's Lottie, too'.

'Nurse Taylor? What's the problem?'

'She's petrified. Since those bastards in Infectious Diseases poached her in 1981, she's forgotten everything. Could you do an *aide memoire* for her? The shortest of short. Say, condition, treatment and emergence of AIDS risk?'

'Why me?'

'My scribe,' he jerked his head back in Margery's direction, 'has gone on strike. Nothing fancy, just the basics, eh? Remember, warmth was always Dottie Lottie's strong point, she was full-bodied but not very full-brained.'

Then he winked. Actually, I now think it was a tic, as he did it twice when pontificating about the Protein Fractionation Centre. Soon, the oppressive heat of the den began to get the better of me; yawning and excessive blinking was turning to sleep. Luckily, the bolshie scribe then teetered in with mugs of tepid black coffee rattling on a tray for us, and all but went arse over tit on the way out of the room, catching her foot on a distinctly mothy kilim.

[sheet stapled to diary]

COPY –

Haemophilia A is a bleeding disorder. The sufferer's blood is deficient in a protein (known as Factor VIII) necessary for the normal clotting process. Without sufficient Factor VIII prolonged bleeding may occur; serious consequences, including death, may follow from internal bleeding into the brain or gut.

Up until the 50s treatment was bed-rest or, sometimes, transfusion with blood or plasma. By the '50s plasma could be separated into its component parts and by the 60s treatment with cryoprecipitate began. Cryoprecipitate was the solid residue left when frozen plasma was thawed. It had been found to contain high levels of Factor VIII. Combining the cryoprecipitate from between 10 to 15 plasma donations provided sufficient Factor VIII to stop haemorrhages. However, it had to be administered in hospital.

The next advance in treatment was through the use of Factor VIII concentrates. They were being commercially produced in the USA and the UK by the 70s. Concentrates had many advantages over cryoprecipitate and the lives of haemophiliacs treated with them became much easier and their life expectancy almost normal.

The concentrates were made from pooled blood donations. A single batch, manufactured in Scotland by the NHS, might require the pooling of 3–4,000 donations. Batches in the USA could be made from ten times as many donations. Concentrates, made from large pools of donated blood, were known to carry a risk of transmitting blood-borne viruses such as hepatitis. The larger the pool, the larger the risk.

In 1981 reports from America of homosexual men suffering from either a rare form of pneumonia or a rare type of cancer (Kaposi's sarcoma) and, in both cases, impaired immune function, were being published in the medical press. Both the cancer and the form of pneumonia were opportunistic infections, i.e. infections taking advantage of a weakened immune system. By the end of the year a homosexual man (a known traveller to the USA) in the UK was discovered to have developed the same syndrome, as had an intravenous (IV) drug user in the USA. By mid-1982 three haemophiliacs in the USA were found to have the same rare form of pneumonia. By the end of 1982 there was a report of what appeared to be a case of AIDS (Acquired Immune Deficiency Syndrome) in a 20-month-old child in San Francisco. The child had received multiple blood transfusions.

That evening, I began to reacquaint myself with the precise chronology of the earliest haemophilia treatments, but little went in and within less than an hour I was too exhausted to read further. After a couple of whiskies, I took my courage in my two hands and phoned Ken. Having discussed his snowdrop collection and, in code, the miseries resulting from prostate treatment, I moved on to our knowledge of the problem of cross-contamination with the AIDS virus of the donation pools. One bag with the virus infecting the whole bally lot. 'Tainted Blood', in short. Just to see what he might say, I also asked him about the regime in Aberdeen. Perhaps not unexpectedly, if my provisional diagnosis of Lewy body dementia is correct, he can recall almost nothing of any significance about it, despite the fact that it was his own show. HE was the man in charge. But he said, with no apparent recollection of the fate of Hitler's underlings, that he simply 'obeyed orders'. Rather pathetically, he appears to imagine that this will save him, repeating it *ad nauseam* to me. As if that was not bad enough he was prepared to assent to all sorts of gibberish I punted. Testing again, I observed how fortunate it was in Scotland that we did not require to give our patients the American stuff. 'Oh, I did,' he replied, airily, apparently blithely unaware of the significance of what he was saying, 'I used it all the time. Our NHS stuff was cheaper, of course, but I used it as and when.'

Poppycock, utter poppycock! Thank God, those sorts of questions will be fired at the Scottish Blood Transfusion Service people, the suppliers and makers of the stuff, and not the likes of us. Their records will tell the truth. Nonetheless, the man is a danger to himself and others. He still sounds normal but he is not normal.

When we were Senior House Officers together, Ken was a beautiful Lothario, seducing every nurse in the Home. They christened him Dr 'Hot Lips'. The last time I looked at him, I shuddered. In his features I recognised my own: tiny, lifeless eyes, bird's beak and bones with parchment stretched across them. Together, we'd look like some anthropologist's collection of shrunken heads. Dr 'No Lips' nowadays.

When I challenged Darling Irma with her failure to water my plants, she said I had not asked her to do so. She also told me, with unexpected vehemence, that it was me who had put the butter in the breadbin! My riposte was that I had found my Gentleman's Relish in the oven. Smiling, knowing it disarms me, she tried, as she habitually does, to engage me in conversation using a previously successful lure, memories of the late lamented Lucky. I did not take the bait, firstly, because tears come to my eyes at the thought of my old chum and, secondly, because chatter-time is then substituted for work-time, and, as she leaves, I discover that my pills have not been laid out or my bed cover turned over.

These free council helper ladies are all very well but I think I shall advertise for a private helper. If I ask Darling Irma to as much as iron my shirt she declines, charmingly, on the grounds that she is a 'Carer' not a daily help. A butcher would have less meaty forearms. Rough Andrea, who comes at night to get me supper and help me undress, parrots the same nonsense. I will advertise in the *Scotsman* for a factotum. I cannot face the Inquiry on my own, I have over three hundred files, the contents of which need to be examined, précised, filleted, put back into chronological order, catalogued and re-filed. I can hardly open the study door, as two have already splurged their innards onto the floor. I do dislike using a biro but have no choice as Rough Andrea has mislaid my fountain pen.

BP 155/91

20th February 2014

Today I held a beauty contest. Actually, the one who reminded me of the young Kay Kendall did not win because she has no 'O' levels, or whatever they are now called. My factotum-to-be is a spinster lady, probably a little over one third of my own great age and her name is Jean Whitadder. She is rosy-cheeked, reads the *Mail* and does not want a full-time job because she plans to write, is doing a 'Creative Writing' course. An ex-librarian to boot. Maybe she will be able to help me on the computer? 'Of course,' she says, she is 'a digital native'. Was I ever an analogue native, I muse? Her first task was to revive the plants and, to my delight, she deliberately watered-off the white fly. My scarlet begonia is spotless. I now have a trio of helpers.

After she left I realised who she reminded me of. Eurovision's Dana, of 'All kinds of Everything' fame. Same heavily lashed eyes, Irish colouring and petite build. Taller than me now, but not when I was in my prime.

My house is like a fridge.

I am no longer sleeping well. As I try to drop off, I begin to rehearse how I will respond to questions from some imaginary, but oh so fierce, QC. After a couple of minutes of self-cross-examination, my striped pyjamas are wringing with sweat and my BP sky-rockets. One question always floors me. Not because I do not know the answer, but because the answer is so complex, requires sophisticated consideration and a clear head. The QC, towering over me with his black gown flapping, resembling a giant crow, says:

'So, Professor Anstruther, on what date did you become aware that the Factor VIII you were prescribing to your haemophiliac patients, made from pooled blood donations, might be contaminated by the AIDS virus?'

I quiver, literally quiver. Does my awareness start when I learn that some new illness in the USA is affecting that clutch of gays, drug addicts and haemophiliacs? Or does it come when I learn of the possibility of transmission here, thanks to Laker's cheap transatlantic flights? With awareness that this disease might be blood-borne and, oh so crucially, a virus, capable of infecting others . . . everyone, wiping out the whole of mankind? With awareness that the citizens of Scotland are all encouraged to donate their blood, nuns and junkies alike? A gift acceptable from anyone. Or the above in some combination, or all together, perhaps?

Then I panic about the meaning of the word 'might'. What does the probability of contamination have to be? Winning the lottery twice, being struck by lightning, a hole in one or being born with red hair?

The QC waits for me to reply, clicking his knuckles like Karenin, eyes never leaving mine. Once I was silver-tongued – well, maybe brass-tongued – articulate, confident. Language was my forte. I addressed symposiums in echoing halls and broke no sweat doing so. Now it refuses to come at my command, hides, proffers meaningless sounds that pass, until they trip off my tongue, as meaningful. Even made-up polysyllabic drug names, the bane of the profession, once held no fear for me. Now, I confuse lose and loose, forget my own telephone number.

I despair.

I must produce a little list for myself (and Ken?) to memorise on why Factor VIII was so much better, until the emergence of AIDS, than the treatment it replaced (cryo-precipitate), so life-changing for my patients.

CRYOPRECIPITATE
  – Painful administration
  – Could only be administered in hospital
  – Long preparation time (1–2 hrs)

- Difficult to administer to children
- Unpleasant side-effects
- Used only once a bleed had begun

FACTOR VIII
- Fairly painless administration
- Home therapy
- No preparation time required
- Easy to administer to children
- Few side-effects
- Prophylactic use

I must devise a mnemonic for each one, the lewder the better as time has proved old Prof Devine right. Smut sticks.

Tonight, before the Inquiry has even begun, a couple of house bricks were thrown through my windows, presumably by one or more of the victims or their relatives? I heard some high-pitched shouting outside, then one flew past me, almost grazing my ear. I dropped my empty sherry glass on the drawing-room floor. Thoughtfully, to simulate blood, the bricks had been dipped in some kind of red dye. I forwent a bath and set Rough Andrea to scrub the carpet. Housework, undoubtedly, but she did not decline. My fawn Axminster now has two pink patches. The police lady on the phone, sounding like a Geordie, showed scant interest in the crime and someone MAY come to speak to me tomorrow. Is this the Bad Blood Brigade stepping up their campaign of harassment? Christ knows, their threatening letters make my blood run cold already. What will I say to the Police, if they do come? Nothing is simple. Every day I feel my strength waning, like snow under summer's sun. I am far too old to fight back.

BP 158/91

23rd February 2014
Thanks to Jean and her computer 'skills' I can now 'copy and paste' onto a Word document. She has made me a card with instructions on it. As advised by her, we now have a printer machine too. I will staple everything I print from the Word into my journal. For, 'In the beginning was the Word'!

Having opened another poison pen letter from my most regular 'Bad Blood Brigade' correspondent, I felt, I have to admit, ill with anxiety. My heart battered my ribs, and my vision began pulsating, in some extraordinary way, with each beat. I caught sight of myself in the hall mirror and did a double-take. A semi-bald, white-faced imp with Ribena-coloured lips seemed to be staring back at me.

In their customary fashion, they address me as 'Murderer'. With the Inquiry looming into view, they are, I suspect, redoubling their efforts in an attempt to rattle me. It works. As I touched the envelope, my neck muscles went into spasm and my bowels turned to liquid (N.B. no Senokot tonight). Nauseous, I took myself off to bed and Jean did a number of useful filing tasks for me. All my correspondence with the Scottish National Blood

Transfusion Service (1970–1990) is now in chronological order and events, decisions, staff re-organisations etc, should appear more choate and comprehensible. She is a treasure. I will save her purely for 'office' work, Irma and Andrea can attend to the more menial tasks.

Jean complains about the cold. She has little on, a pelmet for a skirt. Perhaps I should turn the heating up on the days she comes? Sometimes I suspect that I become, like the tortoise in winter, a bit torpid myself.

I showed her a couple of extracts from my family pedigree book (Mackenzie of Lochail and Campbells of Inverdon). She scanned them into my printer. I've tried an experiment, myself, with another extract relating to my maternal great, great grandfather Bad Old Boswell, a rum cove, and should now be able to 'copy and paste' it. Let's see.

OSSIAN BOSWELL (1811–1881)
9th of Merdiston and of Gruinbank
1811 Born on 22nd October
Educated at Eton and All Souls College, Oxford.

1833 About this year he bought the estate of Gruinbank in Ross-shire, from Mackenzie 6th of Gruinbank, a cadet of Mackenzie of Strathire.

This was an immense estate of some 88,000 acres and included a very fine deer forest and some superb salmon rivers. He seems to have spent much of his life at Gruinbank and there are many references to his eccentricities in a book called 'Old Highland Characters' by Adair, published by John Murray in 1919.

The following are some extracts:

On p. 112 Boswell is described as 'An oddity, an ancient Sassenach who owned many thousands of acres, 45 or 50,000 of which included the best deer ground in Scotland . . . he was magnificently wealthy, by repute, but customarily dressed himself like an old Highland 'puir bodie' or beggar.'

When a stag shot by a neighbour on his own ground reached Gruinbank House on one occasion, Boswell is described as follows:

'The old fellow came to the portal himself. He was clad all in ragged, faded tartan but sported an embroidered Moroccan fez on his head, the many gems on it glittering in the sunlight. Protruding from his muddy, red and white hose was an oversized sgian-dubh. Spying the stag, he ordered two of his servants to convey it to his kitchens and, as if by way of thanks for the gift, gave several cheers for himself and tossed the garron a carrot. He then departed to his own quarters, having bestowed no notice whatsoever upon the donor.'

On p. 132 it is described how 'he attended an assembly in the area, drank unaided the entire contents of the punch bowl before demanding to dance with his host's son, a bachelor of a mere nineteen, in a fashionable quadrille. The other guests remonstrated, but were unable to dissuade him from this course of action. Having completed the quadrille to his own satisfaction, he departed the room, tossing coinage to those gathered outside and demanding "a final fling" from a one-legged beggar woman.'

On p. 156 it describes how he tried to drain a loch on his estate, called Loch Na Beiste, as it was reputed by his tenants to house a monster or water kelpie. He appeared in a caricature in *Punch* at this time because of this venture. Having overlooked the existence of the loch inlet, he failed to drain the loch and it is reported that in his annoyance he fined each of his tenants £1. He then sent his yacht, called 'The Gorgon' to Broadford in Skye for lime, which he poured hot into the loch to poison the beast. Many months later, to the loud cheers of his tenantry, he pulled an old pony carcass out of the water, claiming success 'in ridding the Glens of the Kelpie'.

1834 Succeeded to Merdiston.

1876 In the West Highland Museum in Fort William there is on exhibition a pair of his red and white hose which it is recorded were knitted for him in 1876 by Mrs MacNair of MacNair. They were deposited in the museum by his granddaughter the Hon. Mrs Ursula Donaldson.

1851 The census lists all the inhabitants of Merdiston.

'Ossian Boswell – head of family – aged 40 – Land and Coal Proprietor – Married – Employs 60 labourers, 54 coal miners, 90 boys.'

1868 Involved in a law suit in the Court of Session (McGregor v. Boswell) regarding an attempt by Ossian Boswell to erect a 40 ft statue on his neighbour's demesne. The statue was to portray himself on horseback in the likeness of the god, Mars.

1878 The list of his estates is given in 'Great landowners' by John Bateman, published in 1878.

Ross-shire................ 88,800 acres – £2,463
Lancs.......................2,398 acres – £14,130
Dorset............................755 acres – £618
Yorks West Riding............598 acres – £956
Wilts...............................314 acres – £405

There is some mystery about his marriage which has not been cleared up. He had not less than twelve children but they do not all seem to have had the same mother.

1883 He died at Huntingdon on 16th March, aged 72 years. There were rumours that he was murdered.

BINGO! It came out perfectly. I wish I had learnt to do that years ago, the computer can even do footnotes. To my surprise, Jean was interested in my family. I explained that I was the last of the line, had no antecedents or descendants left. An aged orphan, you could say. She gave me a cuddle. She smells of lemons.

As the last of the line, perhaps, I should compile an entry for myself?

Unable to sleep, I have begun to reread *The Little Prince*. Maybe it will, in its sentimental way, comfort me. No policeman has come.

BP 151/90

1st March 2014

An ashen-faced Jimmy Ward called, uninvited, whilst I was otherwise occupied in the W.C. He has been summoned to attend the Inquiry and tells me that Ken phoned him, in a panic, to say that he has to appear too. I wonder where my summons is? Jimmy said that he has been boning-up to the best of his ability, reminding himself of all the crucial dates, decisions, personnel, tests, results etc for his patients, all set against the history of HIV/AIDS. I reassured him that I had tried to do the same. I did not have the heart to confess my own deficits, I can hardly bear to admit them to myself. With or without a compass, this ship must sail. But nobody can be expected to remember everyday events stretching back over forty years, can they?

It is all in the papers. Relax, everything is somewhere.

But where exactly will I find the document on which I recorded the amount of cryoprecipitate (instead of Factor VIII) we used in the years when the HIV/AIDS risk was the greatest? I must check, again, that twelfth pile by the elephant's foot in the library. Thinking about it, even if I can fish them out, how do I begin to work out the number of patients who would have died over the period from cerebral bleeds before they reached hospital for the cryoprecipitate treatment, if we'd used it instead of Factor VIII? The point is they didn't die! Jimmy said he's done it for his area, but Margery was shaking her head behind his back. Was the shaking attributable to essential tremor, Parkinson's or eloquent of doubt? Who knows. Maybe Prof Eileen will help, numbers have always been her greatest strength (people, less so). Equally, nobody can calculate now, every price having changed over the decades, the cost of buying the additional fridges and centrifuges required for in-hospital cryoprecipitate therapy, can they? Jimmy can't expect that, his own figures can only be a guess at best, whatever he may claim.

Rough Andrea smashed my favourite mug. In my annoyance, I accused her of taking my watch too. Saying nothing, she went to my cutlery drawer, took it out and handed it to me. Really, I have enough on my plate without her tricks.

I spent the evening going through my Royal Hospital papers and some of those from the Infirmary. Nineteen piles. A little while ago, I pictured my mind as an expensive safe, later as a fine-meshed sieve, now I picture it as a colander, a funnel even. I read but retain nothing. Yesterday, for a minute or two, I could not remember exactly how to get home from the Co-op. I am overtired, overwrought. Even if I can find those answers, by tomorrow I will have forgotten that I ever looked for them.

On the bright side, Jimmy and the others have agreed with the methodology I proposed for the collating of HIV patients in Scotland in the early 80s. Health Protection Scotland will provide us with extracts from death certificates. My worry is that, as no one in the early days and, on reflection now, quite possibly, wanted HIV/AIDS on the death certificate, we may grossly underestimate the number of haemophilia patient deaths caused, or contributed to, by HIV/AIDS. Foolishly, I mentioned this on the phone to Ken. Taking me aback, he said 'Jolly good thing too' and then added, cryptically, 'I'm planning on having the Arbroath smokies, they may be in short supply.' He'd returned to our earlier conversation about the HRS lunch.

To my surprise, I find that I like talking to myself, or, more accurately I suppose, writing for myself. I never had a diary, other than for work, I now rather regret that. It is an oddly companionable exercise, soothes me sometimes and helps me get my thoughts in order.

Lucky's ashes were returned in a cardboard urn, the little plaque unluckily commemorating the passing of Lucy. Thinking about it now, is it a typo or the wrong dog? The weight tells me nothing, ashes are ashes. Perhaps my sweet is now killing some newly planted floribunda in Portobello, and an imposter's cluttering up my wardrobe. She will have the benefit of the doubt.

BP 156/92

3rd March 2014

A letter arrived in a small brown envelope looking, to all the world, like an old-fashioned bill. Careless as to its contents, unprepared, I opened it at breakfast.

I have scanned it.

1st March 2014

Dear Professor Anstruther,

This is to give you notice that I have, today, been to the Inquiry premises in order to give a statement. To be frank, speaking to them, after all this time, was like a dream come true for me. I, and the rest of the BBB, have waited so long to tell our side of the story and, I must admit, many times, lost faith, believing that we would never get the chance, and you, and the others, would never be called upon to answer for your actions.

I told them right out that under your Haemophilia care, my husband, Patrick Strowan, had become infected with the AIDS virus. I also told them that before he died my poor husband infected me. As you may imagine, I xplained that if he had known that he had AIDS he would have moved heaven and earth to ensure that he passed that awful disease on to no one. But, as you are aware, he did not know – because you did not tell him. So, this is to inform you that the story is out and now, at last, you will have to account for what you did. Have you prepared your explanation? Is there such a thing? If not, you have only days left before your reputation is destroyed.

I look forward to hearing you in Court.

Maria Strowan

PS For reasons known to themselves, the Inquiry chose to call my Patrick 'Dennis'. Personally, I'd prefer everyone to know what you did to my man. After all, he is the innocent party. He doesn't need anonymity any more, but I am afraid you may well do after all of this is over. My husband thought you were his friend, he trusted you. How wrong he was.

Patrick was my friend. Irma found me in tears and, baffled that I'd not confide in her, got me a cup of tea. How can I explain? I tried to phone Jimmy but he was out. I have no one to speak to, no one who understands and, sometimes, I begin to doubt myself. If I could have given my life to save theirs, I would have long ago. But I go on living and living and living. Living and remembering.

If ever I speculated about the existence of a connection between the nervous system and the bowels I no longer do. I am my own proof.

BP 158/95

15th March 2014
The call has come.

BP 160/95

20th March 2014

Another letter, this time from Oliver Kurtz. Adrian, his twin brother, was amongst the first of my patients to die. I remember his mother assuring him as he lay terminally ill that a cure would be found in time, and begging me with her eyes to collude. I nodded, though I knew it was a lie. Sometimes, in my dreams, I see Adrian. He's twenty, the same age as when he died, standing by the road with his thumb out. Usually I am driving a huge lorry and he begs for a lift and I nod, but as I draw up beside him, take my foot off the accelerator, put it on the brake, the juggernaut judders on past him and I turn around and shout, explaining that it won't stop. 'I've tried!' I say. Looking in the side mirror I see a silhouetted figure with his fist raised high.

I wonder if someone is co-ordinating this campaign?

Reading Oliver's words, I threw up. In the children's clinic, the nurses couldn't tell them apart, but I always knew because Adrian had a microscopic mole in the shape of a bumble bee by his right eye. They thought I had magic powers, called me Dr Who, as I never made a mistake. Nowadays, I doubt I'd be able to see a real mole, any more than it would see me. If I had had a child, I would have liked him to be like Adrian.

25th March 2014

Today I got Jean to collate the policy papers I submitted to my blood transfusion colleagues on blood donor selection as the AIDS crisis progressed. Plucking a letter at random, I was encouraged to see that I'd stuck my neck right out and highlighted the risks from collecting prison blood by as early as 1983! I was in the van there, got some stick from the Howard League, the Governors and their tame civil servants. But the statistics, on hepatitis alone, made them back off.

In a postscript, I also suggested they banned homosexuals and IV drug users from giving their blood. Triumphantly, I showed the letter to Jean, expecting praise, but she looked blank.

'You a homophobe? Why pick on them?' she asked, busy poaching an egg for me.

'Why . . . ?' I spluttered. How can people have forgotten so quickly? 'Because all the early reports of symptoms were in homosexual men, then intravenous drug users . . . you know, needle-sharers.'

'Why them?'

'Because, although we didn't know it then, AIDS is a blood-borne virus . . . spreads through blood . . . and blood products. Gay men were treated like lepers – shunned, reviled as plague carriers . . .'

'Righto, calm your farm, Prof!'

Calm your farm?

Although she remained unimpressed, frankly I impressed myself, as I had no recollection whatsoever of having done any of this. Particularly as some other papers showed that the Health Department itself only changed their policy in '83 and, interestingly, the shiny, new AIDS-era leaflet that they produced to give to potential donors stated 'Can AIDS be transmitted by transfusion of blood and blood products? Almost certainly yes.' Apparently, they'd made their minds up. Yet the press release with it included, shamefully, the usual line the government pedalled at the time, i.e. that there was 'no conclusive proof' that the disease was transmitted by blood or blood products. So those intending to give blood were given one message, and the public, and those using blood products like my haemophiliacs, were still being told quite another.

God forbid that I should have to square that circle, reconcile those two. Sport will be had at the Inquiry with some Home Office bigwig, unless he's fortunate enough to be dead.

Jean likes pink, she often wears it and, no doubt having washed my clothes with hers, my white hankies are now a fetching puce.

List for Irma:
- Green bananas
- Paracetamol
- Stamps
- Post-it notes
- Chicken pie

Unlike before, last time Irma did the shopping she did not give me any receipts, just some old bits of till paper. She says she has, but I am no longer sure that she is completely trustworthy. Jimmy Ward's son rang me to tell me that his mother, Margery, had died. Sad news, but I don't think I've set eyes on her for years. In her prime she was a dusky beauty, sought after way beyond the physiotherapy department. Atheists, the pair of them, so, with luck, a memorial ceremony at worst, or, better still, just a quick do in the Crem? I wonder if Jimmy will be granted some sort of stay of execution *vis à vis* the Inquiry?

Thank God I found Jean. I can rely upon her, if none of the others. A cut above the rest. I may, I'm not sure yet, let her draw money out for me as the bank's so far from the shops. She says I could use 'another hole in the wall', but I've no idea what she means. Today I dictated a letter to her and she helped me sign it. My signature, once a tight little huddle of letters, is now, thanks to my tremor, more like that of some exuberant third-rate artist, with big loops and ludicrous downstrokes. What would a graphologist make of that? Am I a changed man?

I have discovered that she has a child, is one of those 'single Mums', I suppose. I think he's called Garry and she says he's a 'big baby'. He likes trains.

This evening Rough Andrea told me, in a casual, conversational way, that she is heavily in debt and can no longer get any loans. Both the cards are 'max-ed out' and her Mum's skint. Her rent is due at the end of the month, apparently. As I was fingering my supper sandwiches, wondering vainly what to say, she jumped to the antics of her daughter's nipper, Kyle. I have always taken a great interest in him as he is a haemophiliac, has quite severe Haemophilia A, I deduced. Once I tried to explain to her that she must be a carrier, like Queen Victoria, that it comes out almost exclusively in males but only passes down the female line. I said Kyle shared his condition with the little Tsarevich, Alexei. But she wasn't a bit interested, shut me up by saying, firmly, that her tubes had been tied.

Because I am so decrepit and sometimes, I suspect, a little wandery, I expect she thinks I am, was, little more than a jumped-up paramedic or GP. Jean, by way of contrast, loves to hear about my 'old' days, asks me endless questions about them, and seemed genuinely impressed when I told her about my Fulbright scholarship, Princeton medal and the Chair endowed in my name. I wonder why she never married? She is certainly pretty enough, with her peaches and cream colouring.

I have had a front door key cut for her and presented it to her on a little cushion, probably one of my mother's ancient, and now scentless, lavender bags. She curtsied prettily as she accepted it.

Irma, or Rough Andrea, is rearranging my furniture at her whim. Where have they put my candlesticks, Granny McNeill's silver teapot with her crest on it and my pair of Georgian salt-cellars? To cap it all, while fishing fresh pyjamas out of my drawer I found a plastic bag with lamb's kidneys in it. Is this some kind of joke?

11th April 2014

With blotches parading down my cheek, I have shingles and they are agony. I sat on the edge of the bath and Jean shaved me, meticulously manoeuvring around them. A trained nurse could not have taken more tender care. In the cold, I couldn't stop shivering, chittering. Bed is the only warm place in this house. I don't like my downstairs bedroom, miss my grandparents' four-poster and the portrait in pastels of my mother. Even when I was little, I always slept upstairs, although the nursery was downstairs. Upstairs, I feel safer, out of harm's way. Here any Tom, Dick or Harry can poke his nose in, break my window and assault me.

All the time the clock is ticking but I feel too weak, too ill, to prepare myself for the Inquisition. While I was in bed listening to the radio the usual afternoon play came on. It was about Harold Shipman. I had to switch it off.

On Tuesday last, I got another of those vile letters and, not for the first time, I was compared to that man. His 'antics', apparently, 'pale' beside mine. Between the pain, my constant fatigue and this new, perpetual sense of impending doom, rendering the loosening qualities of lactulose otiose, I found myself weeping out loud. I couldn't stop.

For some reason, my imagination transported me to the 'support' group that Annie Taylor and I set up in 1985. Every month we met up with those of our haemophilia patients who had contracted AIDS through the Factor VIII I had prescribed. I repeat, I PRESCRIBED. Month after month new symptoms emerged, month after month our membership dwindled through death until, out of the original 22 of us, there was only Annie, me, Graeme and Simon. Simon, whom I had treated since he was six months old, was dying in front of my eyes and Graeme looked not far behind. That was our last meeting. I wished then, and wish to this day, that my life could have been taken instead of theirs. I feel I have their blood on my hands. Christ, forgive me.

A chiropodist, yet another new one, rang my bell and said a home visit for me had been fixed at the clinic. By whom, I forbore to inquire? In accordance with my usual practice, I asked the little girl (Stacey), for that is what she was, how many bones there are in the human foot? '26,' she replied, and as she was correct I let her at me with her pointed implements. I sent the last one away. Stacey chatted like a budgerigar and it turns out that this child has two children of her own. She told me, pouting in indignation, that her last customer, a below-the-knee amputee, had asked if he'd be half price.

BP 153/92

13th April 2014

I had two visitors today, one invited and one uninvited. The doorbell woke me, fortunately, at 2.30 p.m. from a sleep I was having in my chair. A young man from the Royal College arrived (I'd forgotten about his visit) to discuss a portrait they want of me for the Physicians Hall. In my drawing room, I gave him the photo of me at the Palace, taken when I was the President, and, crucially, looked semi-human, but the fellow insisted the woman painter wants to do it from life. I am to 'sit'. He handed me a leaflet showing some of her commissions and a couple of her works, housed in the National Gallery.

'But I am a ghoul now,' I mused and at that the fellow, agreeing, I have little doubt, lost the power of speech. Actually, having seen the works of the chosen portraitist I have little to worry about. Her work is so abstract that I was unable to distinguish Richard Dawkins' features from 'Self-portrait: sunbathing in the nude, Skye'.

My second caller was a be-suited man, carrying leaflets in one hand, who slipped effortlessly through the open door while I was attempting to keep him at bay. I followed him into my kitchen where, without my permission, he sat down and took his overcoat off. I was, I must admit shaking, scared that he might be one of my unknown BBB correspondents come to assault me. Was I 'looking forward to my resurrection to be with Christ?' he asked.

Recognising him as a Jehovah's Witness and hugely relieved, I explained that, not yet being dead, I felt that death was a more pressing concern.

As a representative of a sect I abhor, I did not feel the need to offer him tea. In less than ten minutes the cold had got the better of him and he looked enviously at my three pullovers, unaware of the double vests below them. In order to expedite his exit, I mentioned that my entire professional life had been concerned with blood, blood product ingestion, transfusions, etc, and my tactic worked like a dream. Had I been Dracula himself he could not have looked more appalled.

I declined his offer of prayer and I doubt he'll trouble me again.

14th April 2014

Irma let me know that she was cross with me by slamming plates down on the kitchen table in front of me, making my fork jump in the air, and saying as little as she possibly could. My cufflinks are missing, that is a fact. She puts my shirts in the wash, that is a fact. She takes them out, that is a fact. Methinks the lady doth protest too much. They were gold and had the University crest on them.

The ear person, Kevin, came and turned up the volume in my right aid. It, as I had predicted, made not the slightest difference as my ear drum is thick with impacted wax. Will they syringe, or 'skoosh' as Kevin says, my ear? No, they won't, in case I get tinnitus. I already have tinnitus. I am no longer in control of my destiny. He asked me, chattily, about the abundance of paperwork on the drawing-room floor and remarked, on leaving, that H and S at his work would have something to say if they knew that the place was 'like a tinderbox'. Will I be blacklisted? How am I going to answer questions at the Inquiry if I cannot hear?

As arranged, I went to tea with Prof. Eileen Coates. Though only about nine years younger than me she is still a good-looking woman. Her thickset daughter, Bridget, with whom she lives, hovered discreetly in the background; vigilant, I think, that I should not overtire her mother. Bridget was, as ever, head to foot in tweed; I feel the island of Harris owes her a great debt. I apologised for my lateness, explaining that my Polish taxi-driver seemed unfamiliar with the New Town and seemed to enjoy our tour of Moray Place, Great Stuart Street and Heriot Row.

In her cosy nest, we discussed the joint paper she, Jimmy, Gavin and I are producing. Competent as ever, she is already ahead with the statistical analysis. She asked how Ken was holding up, told me that he has phoned her several times, invariably in a fever of anxiety, repeating himself and asking semi-imbecilic questions.

E.g. 'Will they take into account the number of students I taught, now spread throughout the western world?' (Verbatim.)

One bit of good news, though I've no idea how she discovered it, is that Prof. Mick Horner of the BMA is to give expert evidence to the Inquiry on the medical ethics aspect. What an untold relief! Both she and I had been worried sick that with some tin-pot, touchy -feely man we'd find ourselves judged by the standards of this new patient/customer age. In the old days, by mutual consent, mind, we were Gods, Gods in pinstripes. We made the decisions, bore the worry. Nowadays everyone is a consumer and wants to know everything, whether they can understand it or not. In the old days, we protected them, bore the burden of fear for them. Or, at least, that's what we all thought. Nowadays, the petrified patient must be told 'it' might be terminal, even if that ruins their last few weeks upon the earth, despite the fact 'it' might turn out to be benign.

The consultant who excised my benign growth a couple of years ago wore plimsolls, stripy socks and a T-shirt at our first meeting. To meet him, I wore a suit. Does he break 'The News', if it is bad, in that attire?

When I asked Eileen how the wait before the thing

begins was affecting her she shrugged it off. An impressive woman, but a cold fish. After less than three-quarters of an hour, the daughter appeared, my greatcoat slung over her arm, and none too subtly assisted me to my feet. I was, in all honesty, exhausted and Eileen looked deathly pale. She didn't get up from her chair.

As Bridget and I were waiting in the street for my taxi to pull up, I noticed a black car that appeared to have had a pot of thick red gloss poured over its roof. 'Mine,' Bridget said, scuffing some dog muck off her brown brogues onto the pavement edge. 'It happened last night. Mummy no longer drives, she gave it to me, but it was outside our door and they'll have thought it was hers. It's happened before.'

'The Bad Blood Brigade?'

She nodded. 'Who else? Someone from the CID is supposed to be looking into it. Are they pestering you too?'

I nodded but found that I could not say anything.

Sometimes I feel I am on another planet.

Jean came promptly at 7.30, she's a stickler (like me) for punctuality. I think it's a hereditary trait. I caught the slightest scent of violets, 'my shampoo,' she said, pleased that I had noticed. We tried to do some more cataloguing but I was not up to it, became sufficiently muddled for her to remark on it in an admirably direct fashion. If I cannot get my correspondence with the Protein Fractionation Centre arranged, how will I know what I was thinking? Eventually, she helped me to bed and, unasked, brought me a mug of 'Hot Chocolate'. I did not know I had such stuff in my cupboards. It was cloyingly sweet but I drank it all down to please her, skin and all. Tomorrow, without fail, I must get Irma to throw the filth out.

15th April 2014

Hearing raised voices coming from my bedroom, I went there as a red-faced Andrea stormed past me murmuing darkly about 'that woman' and 'telling them in the office'. Jean, apparently unmoved, carried on wordlessly with her allotted task, simply widening her eyes at me in recognition of the incident. I fled. In harnessing three females I may have overreached myself, forfeited all peace. At the Free, a student nurse of my acquaintance, a harp-playing Hungarian, yanked the hair of a colleague whom she considered had made eyes at 'her' man, Philip Harman. Phil told me he'd never as much as exchanged a word with 'the little plucker', as he called her.

23rd April 2014

Today I went to Learmonth House, a faux-Adam building inserted into a gap in a New Town crescent. The taxi driver, another Pole, helped me with my bag of papers up the stairs at the front. A kind, matronly civil servant escorted me to the interview room and, unasked, got me a cup of tea. The room smelt of floor polish. For about, say, an hour and a half, I was questioned by a slight girl, one of the Counsel to the Inquiry, all about some tests I carried out on my haemophilia patients in the early '80s.

Twice, I was distracted at seeing through the glass door some old colleague or other shuffling past, interrogation over. We're like cows, each one being milked in a separate milking parlour. I tried to explain to the youngster how extraordinarily difficult it is to recall now, what I thought in a time of ignorance. Nowadays, when AIDS has been recognised as a blood-borne virus for many decades, so much of what we did, or thought, seems strange, slight, indefensible. She kept returning to the San Francisco child case, the twenty-month-old who, in about 1982, was reported as having something that looked like AIDS and was known to have had multiple transfusions, including from a man found subsequently to have developed AIDS. How did that affect my thinking at the time as to whether AIDS might be a blood-borne virus? I think I thought the child might have had some congenital immune deficiency, I replied; but the truth is I cannot remember what went through my head over thirty years ago. All I know is that, like many of my colleagues, I was not persuaded that it was a blood-borne virus at the time. But why not, she demanded? I have no idea. Once it was thought that maggots were spontaneously generated from dead flesh and many eminent scientists adhered to that belief too, laughable as it might seem now.

Her sceptical look said it all.

My answers in relation to Koch's postulates (as a means of proving that an infectious agent causes a particular illness when transmitted from one person to another) won her unconcealed approbation, following nil expectation I'll be bound. 'Thighs in Tights Titillate', a mnemonic devised by myself, was the secret of my success. A Penguin biscuit was offered to me and as I was working my way through it, hoping my chin was not smeared with chocolate, our session was interrupted. In bowled a near spherical little dandy, my height, in a black jacket as I was mid-crunch, and my questioner seemed both flustered by him and abnormally deferential to him. Chocolate-smeared, I appeared to be invisible to the man. Perhaps it was tact, as I have little doubt that it was the Judge. Jimmy had told me that Goodhart is on the Food Committee of the New Club (rice pudding being his dessert of choice) and that the shine on his shoes could blind you.

As I was waiting for the taxi, distracted, I lost my grip on my bag of papers and the next thing I knew they had spilled into the gutter, some blowing free, somersaulting along the street. A fellow coming out of the same building chased them for me, collected them and stuffed them back into my now mud-spattered carrier. Looking into his face as he returned it, I saw it was Geoffrey Pearson. As ever, with his split-veined cheeks and sturdy frame, he's more like a farmer than the senior tax official that he actually is. I thanked him and, apprehensively, I must admit, inquired how he was keeping. He said, 'Fine, just fine.'

'And you?'

A little too breathless, I said, 'Fine too. Were you giving a statement in there?'

He nodded.

Then, to my surprise, he put one of his huge arms around my shoulder and murmured, 'Don't you worry, Prof, I told them how good you were to us, nothing was too much trouble. My Mum worshipped you.' That boy's AIDS test result was amongst the first positive ones I saw. Tears came to my eyes at his generosity, as they had when I first saw his result, so to hide them I turned away towards the building and when I turned back he had gone, was running to catch a bus. God bless him.

Near home, I got the taxi to stop at a toy shop. For about quarter of an hour, I discussed train sets with a bespectacled youth suffering from a rather disfiguring *nevus flammeus* covering one half of his face. In accordance with his advice, I have purchased a Hornby 'Country Flyer' train set for Garry. It is, I understand, his birthday tomorrow and he and Jean are to go out for a meal to McDonald's restaurant.

Rough Andrea got me my supper and helped me to bed, offering me a sponge for my chocolate-streaked chin. I was so tired that my sausages held no appeal, even chewing felt like a chore. After she had left Bridget Coates rang to say that I had left behind my umbrella and my papers. She is to deliver both tomorrow. What a treasure she is, lucky old Eileen having her. Ken phoned but I did not have the energy to speak to him, far less to comfort him, so I lied and said I'd have to go as someone had come to my door. Will Lord Goodhart recognise him for what he is, a confused, foggy shadow of his former self? Somewhere inside that shambling wreck is the choirboy who sang a solo at the Coronation. If only the Inquiry had been in the '90s, early 2000s at a pinch. Ken has not been the same since his stroke.

Back to *The Little Prince*, and Katherine Woods' thoughtful translation. It's the passage about the rose and her thorns, which, she maintains, protect her from the claws of the tiger. It tells us that true love remains steadfast despite recognising our imperfections, little lies, exaggerations and vanity. If I had understood that book better sixty years ago I might not be sleeping alone in a narrow hospital bed. That reminds me, Jean is coming in early tomorrow to continue her cataloguing of my papers. I must remember to show her those old files in my wardrobe. I think ours will be a fruitful collaboration as she has an unusually good mind, certainly, for a Carer. I have become accustomed to her face.

If darling Lucky was still alive, it would be her birthday.

Some dissonant jingle on the World Service woke me and I went to the window and looked out over the moonlit loch. The rest of the city was asleep, at peace, and I wished it could be like this forever. I tried to open the sash window but I no longer have sufficient strength in my arms. I have lived too long, and life is becoming a burden.

25th April 2014

I am going to staple in this 'cut and paste' statement used by the Inquiry. Somehow, the marvels of modern technology, they put a transcript of the previous day's evidence on their Web Site. In it are 'links' to documents mentioned during the evidence. I am putting this document here because 'HARRY', (actually, William Donald) was one of my patients and I am bound to be asked something about his treatment. Anonymity sought even now suggests that, despite Princess Di's cuddles, the stigma remains.

STATEMENT OF HARRY
(taken by Eric Abrassard on 12th July 2013)

I am the youngest of three children. When I was born in 1970 we were living in ███████████. When I was only three months my knee began to swell and I was referred to ██████████ hospital. After they'd taken a lot of blood samples, a coagulation screen there revealed that I had Haemophilia A, my Mum says I screamed the roof down whilst they were taking the blood. My Mum and Dad were told nothing about my condition or the treatment (Cryoprecipitate) I was receiving then.

From the age of five, I was treated by Dr Anstruther with Factor VIII for all the bleeds I had. My Mum was taught how to give me injections of it. They hurt. Nowadays, she says she can't forgive herself because she injected the stuff into me. She was the carrier of the Haemophilia, too. I used to go to hospital about every three months to be monitored and to have blood tests. Because of my Haemophilia I had bleeds about once or twice a week but I only needed to go to hospital if they were particularly bad. By the time I was 12 I was injecting myself.

I trusted my doctors, I never questioned the treatment they were giving me.

In about 1984, when I was still 13, a nurse told my mum, in passing, that I was one of the children infected with HIV. My Mum did not know that my blood had been tested for HIV. Mum and Dad were horrified because all they knew about HIV was that it was in Africa and that gay people and druggies had it. They were told to keep my diagnosis a secret. I think the only other person who knew was my GP. My younger sisters weren't told or my grandparents. Mum found it difficult looking as if she didn't have a care in the world. She was always terrified, as was Dad, that someone would learn our secret. Everywhere, on the TV, in the papers, there was stuff about the 'Gay Plague'. Someone thought up an ad about an iceberg, a tombstone rising up with AIDS carved on it and a scary voice saying 'There is now a danger that is a threat to us all. It is a deadly disease and there is no known cure . . .' I've never forgotten it. Can you imagine hearing that off the TV daily, if you're still just a boy and already got the disease? I remember reading something in the Sun saying that AIDS could be caught in a swimming pool if there were any people with AIDS swimming. I used to love swimming but we stopped it then.

My Mum told me about the HIV when I was about 14. I thought I was going to die. They never let my school know as they knew I might not be allowed back or, if I was, I would be treated differently. When I was 16 I had to go to hospital with some kind of infection. I was kept in a side room and everything in it was covered in a sort of polythene so that I couldn't infect it. The nurses wore gowns and masks when they brought me my food. My food was on paper plates so that they could be thrown away when I'd finished. My paper sheets were to be burnt. One day, I remember my mum crying beside me on the bed.

In about 1989 I was put on the Co-trimoxazole trial

but I don't know whether I got the drug or a placebo. In about 1990 the night sweats started. By 1991 I was on AZT, my mouth was sore and I was too skinny to be healthy. Things got worse in 1992 and I'd a cough that wouldn't go away and I'd a horrid rash. To be honest, I was a bit patchy in taking the drugs, you are at that age. By then I was living in digs with a couple and going to college. The couple knew I had Haemophilia. One night there was a radio programme about people with Haemophilia having AIDS. The wife asked me straight out if I had AIDS. I didn't lie and the next day they asked me to find somewhere else to live. I got immunoglobin treatment and in 1997 Lamivudine was added to my AZT. By 1998 I was on triple therapy. I didn't like taking the big tablets and, sometimes, I just skipped them. I can't work because of the arthritis I've got in my joints from bleeds. I've gone blind now from progressive multifocal leukoencephalopathy due to my HIV. By 2004 I was on four drugs and I still am.

My diseases have made me anti-social and not seeing makes life difficult. Carers are in and out of my house day in, day out. I'm never alone. I've never had a girlfriend as I wouldn't know how to tell her.

I was born with Haemophilia. I was not born with AIDS and I don't know exactly when I caught it. But I do know how I caught it. Dr Anstruther kept me on the Factor VIII even when he knew that there was a risk I'd catch AIDS from the stuff. I could have gone back to Cryoprecipitate, the stuff they used to give us before Factor VIII replaced it. Maybe, if I'd been told of the risk,

I'd have taken it. I don't know. All I know was I was not given the choice.

Nothing I did would make the document come up on my computer 'Word' document. I followed my instruction sheet exactly, tried again and again typing in what it said. All the time, I could feel myself sweating, the muscles in my shoulders tightening, pulling on my spine until it ached. Once technology held no fears, excited me, made me a better doctor. I welcomed it with arms open. This, at every turn, defeats me. But if I can't magic up the papers, if I can't read them, what will happen to me? The Inquiry is 'paperless'? I am 90 years old, not an old dog trying to learn new tricks, but one lying prone on the vet's table, blinking, waiting for deliverance.

After about forty minutes' unequal struggle, Jean did it for me. I didn't want her to as I knew she'd look at the thing. When she got up, I felt her looking at me with new, hostile eyes.

'Why didn't you?' she asked.

I tried to explain, that we thought Scottish blood products were safe, that if I'd known I'd have taken everyone off the stuff, that throughout the country doctors everywhere were making the same decision that I did, that the Haemophilia Society were so keen on it they were petitioning the Government not to block American, American mind, imports of the stuff. I took the calculated risk, but the risk was to them. Forgive me, I gibbered, couldn't get my words out. Awfully, I began to cry. It was like my nightmare only worse, and I knew I sounded defensive, incoherent, almost hysterical. Pathetic. As I was sobbing, Jean came and put her arms around me and just held me tight. No one has done that for over sixty years.

Of course, she is paid, they are all paid by someone, but, somehow, I know that she cares. I don't know how I know, but I do. I remember Willy Donald as a fat little boy, we had a jar of lollipops in the clinic and he'd always beg for two.

She said Garry, her little boy, was delighted by my train. I wonder if he looks like her?

26th April 2014
My teeth have gone walkabout.

27th April 2014
My teeth have returned, unrepentant. I found them peering into a jar of gooseberry jam. Honey, I would have understood.

28th April 2014
How clever Jean is! I was napping in my armchair when she arrived, cheeks red from the rush, with a birthday cake, pink piped icing, for me. How on earth did she know?

Eileen phoned at about four o' clock. She said Ken has given his evidence and she thinks, but it may be wishful thinking, that he was so execrably bad that the Inquiry judge cannot have failed to see that his mind has departed this earth before him. Apparently, he nodded his head at what virtually anyone said, assented to contradictory assertions, could produce no figures of his own, mixed up Drs Grey, Kinloch and Goss, and had no recollection of his practices in relation to giving patients their test results, offering them alternative therapies or the quantities involved in his annual orders of Factor VIII for his clinics. He also seemed to have difficulty in reading the screen in front of him in the Inquiry Room, using it, at one stage, as a mirror. How will I cope?

Sandwiches without peanut butter, or any other filling, tonight. I made the elementary error of talking too much to Rough Andrea whilst she was sticking the crusted bits together with margarine (?). I've never asked her to get that foul oil. The trap was laid and I fell straight in, being only too eager to tell her all about the curative effect of a liver transplant in haemophilia but, as I have found out to my cost before, I was cut off before I could explain why, and she rushed out the door murmuring she was late for 'her other lady'.

I will throw out the sandwiches and have more cake instead.

I am too tired to think. Somehow, I have lost an envelope that had almost £500 of cash in it. I kept it in my sock drawer to pay tradesmen in case I could not get to the bank. I muttered something about it to Irma at lunchtime but she did not respond. She heard, though. In bed, I watched some TV but so many of the ads make no sense. What is a Pentel? Also, I am worried that the tin of asparagus soup I finished for supper yesterday was bad. The inside of the lid looked black. My factotum seems to have spirited the little that was left in the consommé can away.

30th April 2014

Jean is doing a very good job indeed. This morning, she has produced three pages of typescript, cataloguing a large part of the contents of what I called Box A. In it were masses of old family letters, my genealogical pamphlets, various citations of my long dead relatives, including Robert's Croix de Guerre and my grandfather's MC. No one will add my various honorary degrees, awards, KBE citation, etc to it. She sometimes asks me questions, listens, and I get the feeling that she is genuinely interested in my family. I am becoming dependent upon her.

Could I cope without her?

Rough Andrea was late for my lunch again. If 'the other lady' asks again to be toileted just as she is about to leave, she should remonstrate with her. My 15 minutes are inadequate as things stand. I asked her age. 75. At that age I could still skip up Schiehallion.

I am just back from the shops, soaking wet, and had a horrible experience. I put various comestibles from the supermarket in my string bag and left to go to the Post Office. As I reached the zebra crossing, a big man grabbed me by the sleeve and, very roughly, began pulling me back to the supermarket, shouting all the while. I fell over onto the wet tarmac. He kept saying that I had not paid. I said that I had. I was taken to the store detective's office and shown film and it seems I did leave without paying. I explained that it was a mistake, that I'd pay now. As I was being led out somewhere again by the burly fellow, Jean saw me and seemed to know the fellow still manhandling me. I don't know what she said, but she screamed at him, harangued him and he unhanded me and hissed, in a very offensive manner, that I was 'not to do it again'. As if I was a three-year-old child.

I am still not sleeping and my taste buds seem to be changing. Usually I like custard, but tonight it tasted bitter.

Once in bed, I wanted to forget the present, knew I could lose myself in the pages of my pedigree book. Whilst I love the romance of it, being descended from Moncrieff of that Ilk, Campbells of Lochawe, the Lord of the Isles (the very names thrill me), I understand only too well that, in many ways, genealogy is a vain and foolish pursuit. Everyone is begat by Someone. I met a puffed-up Herald once who bored me to the edge of my grave, and, in his pomposity, almost turned me communist with his boasts of being a direct descendant of St Moluag. To annoy, I claimed Lucy (Australopithicus) as my own distant aunt, explaining that she was a rather hirsute forebear on my maternal side but with an uncannily strong family resemblance. All of us upon the earth at this moment match each other, more or less, generation for generation. And I, of all people, know that the same red blood flows in all our veins. But, throughout my long life, the truth is that the thought of my forebears has stiffened my spine, propelled me onwards in my career and in my life. As it so happens, none of them to my knowledge were vagrants or rag-and-bone men, and I have not let them down. So far, my reputation is intact. The thought that I might haunts me.

I've noticed that Jean sometimes flicks through the book, always that one, if she's having a sly cup of coffee. The other day she asked me questions about my mother's family and I found myself regaling her with silly family stories, like the time my mother knocked herself right out with a croquet mallet and, somehow, simultaneously got the ball through the hoop. She looked at old photos, seemed particularly keen to see my sister, Isabel. None of the others seem remotely interested. I told her about the art school and so on, the car accident. 'Why's she so much younger than you?' she asked, so I explained about Hector's death and her always being known as the 'Little Mistake'. 'Garry's my mistake,' she said, 'not so little, but I love him to bits.'

I have made a momentous decision. The bloodline has run out and I am as free as a bird. Whilst I still breathe, I will give my possessions to those I wish, rewarding virtue where I see it and being rewarded myself with a smile. I will begin with my mother's ivory sewing kit.

1st May 2014

Floundering, unable to get out of the bath, I had to be helped by Andrea. She brushed aside my embarrassment by saying that she'd seen more 'bits' than a horse, adding, when I looked blank, 'More wands, you know, than Harry Potter?'

How the mighty are fallen.

Irma said she was going shopping on George Street so I asked her to drop off my cleaning, but she declined; apparently, anything other than 'caring' is forbidden by the management. I said if I cared about someone I would drop off their cleaning for them, but she looked blank.

'What about my food?' I said, 'you buy that for me?'

'You need that,' she said.

'I need clean clothes, too.'

'You'll have to speak to the agency,' she replied, closing my front door.

I'll get Jean to do it. She cares. She put cream on my face. I look as if I've swopped blows with Muhammad Ali, one side of my face is swollen, purplish and yellow. My only true carer was, today, rewarded with the sewing kit. I pointed out the minute scissors, stork's legs as the blades. However she seemed underwhelmed by the gift, even when I drew her attention to the hallmarks on the silver.

A man phoned today to talk about windows, kept insisting that I turn my computer on to see if they were going slow. I asked, civilly, in the circumstances, how windows could go slow? Mine open and close adequately, are largely sash and case, although there is one Velux.

'Have you a computer, Sir?'

'Yes.'

'Well, you just go to it and switch it on for me and I'll guide you what to do after that.'

'But my windows are not controlled by my computer,' I said, baffled.

He put the phone down on me.

Andrea says it is a well-known scam. 'Cover the computer up at night with a cloth, otherwise they can watch you undress or whatever,' she cautioned.

They?

Who would want to watch me undress, I asked her?

Unaware that this was a rhetorical question, and, perhaps, in the light of our recent encounter, she gabbled 'Oh, well, I don't know . . . maybe, well . . .' before scurrying off, hand over her mouth.

5th May 2014

Due to my bruises, I can't lean my head on my hand as I read. Nonetheless, I spent a couple of hours looking over the theories, flying about in the early '80s, to do with what was causing AIDS. Some now seem hare-brained. In the mist, the one I favoured, and clung to for too long, now appears absurd even to me. I was convinced that an excess of foreign protein, either from sperm in the case of homosexual men or repeated infusions of Factor VIII in haemophiliacs, led to a state of immune-suppression, and that AIDs was an end stage of such immune abnormalities. How could I believe that? AIDS was new but homosexuality was not. The authors of those scary letters (another came this morning), forget that no one KNEW, so, inevitably, theories abounded. They were all we had. And by the time the mist had cleared, it was already too late for some of my poor patients. Putting it into words, it sounds so glib. But we could hardly have used Koch's postulates on our patients as if they were guinea pigs, could we? Maybe that's what they imagine we did, infect them, purely for the advancement of science? This morning's ugly missive, which came through the Royal Mail, was addressed in red ink to 'The Killer Anstruther' and handed to me by Andrea. Disconcertingly, not so much as an eyebrow was raised on her face despite this unpleasant appellation. Does she believe that is what I am?

Without thinking, while she was peeling my pear in the kitchen, I asked her about the little boy's haemophilia control. She shut me up straight away. It was as if I'd asked her to disrobe. Maybe she's turning against me too, with those letters and the Inquiry coming up.

A leaflet pushed through my letterbox asked if I wished to join a pole-dancing class. If I bring along a friend I am to receive a surprise gift. I wonder if Eileen would oblige?

My face hurts and my jaw clicks when I eat.

6th May 2014

It is decreed. I am to appear at the Goodhart Inquiry on the 15th May. To be grilled for a week, definitely, but maybe for two. It seems that because of Ken's rubbish they want me to fill in as many blanks as I am able about what went on in Aberdeen. I have enough paperwork on the subject but no energy, or inclination, to look them out, pick them up, never-mind read them. I am twelve years older than that man. How I wish this horrid feeling of doom would leave me. From the moment I wake, I feel anxious, uneasy, troubled. It's physical; in the pit of my stomach, rings the base of my skull. Frankly, if I had any tranquilisers I would be sorely tempted to take them, except that I'd feel foggier yet, might accidentally put myself to sleep like lucky old Lucky. It's difficult to think straight when lifting a pen exhausts me. A little pick-me-up of Kendal Mint Cake followed by some whisky might be worth a try.

Irma must get me:
- Green bananas
- Milk
- Chops
- Tenapants
- Kendal Mint Cake.
- Electric razor

[Cutting found in Anstruther's journal]
PARIS COURT CONVICTS THREE FOR HIV-CONTAMINATED BLOOD
by Tranter Baxter

May 2014
PARIS, May. 3—

In Paris today, a court brought in a guilty verdict on a trio of health officials on charges of distributing tainted blood that infected over 1,250 haemophiliacs with the AIDS virus. 273 of those patients are already dead.

The case followed upon an official investigation which concluded that senior health officials had ordered the continued use of the blood-clotting factor, required by those with haemophilia, despite the fact that the officials knew the factor to be contaminated and procedures to detect and destroy the virus were available.

In the dock were Dr Claude Juppé, former head of the National Blood Transfusion Centre, his deputy, Dr Michael Fevrier and Celine Barrat, a Senior Haematological Consultant. All three were sentenced to four years in prison, although Fevrier and Barrat's sentences were suspended for two years. Juppé and Fevrier were also ordered to pay substantial compensation to the AIDS victims and their families.

Juppé and Fevrier were found guilty of 'a fraudulent description of goods' (the charge of poisoning requiring an intent to kill). Many of those infected with the virus, or their families in the case of fatalities, are angry that politicians have not also been charged for their responsibility for the scandal. The deputy health Minister, Raymond St Cloude, amazed the court with his admission that he and others in the government knew that the blood-clotting factor was contaminated more than four months before it was ordered to be withdrawn.

There was uproar in the Palais de Justice this morning when the verdict was announced, relatives of AIDS patients sobbing and one shouting:

'This country, my own state, murdered my child! French justice died with him . . .'

A woman whose 14-year-old haemophiliac son contracted AIDS from the tainted blood said to an interviewer:

'When you take a gun, aim at the head and pull the trigger, you are aware that you have killed, and you go to jail. These people were all aware that they were killing! Four years? For shoplifting maybe. It's enough to make you weep!'

In the trial, none of the health officials were able to explain why the tainted blood was not withdrawn until October 1985, even though in May of that year blood-bank officials knew of the contamination of the blood products used by haemophiliacs. In the verdict issued today the Court said that the accused had deceived the haemophiliacs.

'If fully informed, the haemophiliacs could have made a different decision.'

In May, the accused could have used techniques, then available and used in other European countries such as Scotland, to decontaminate the blood or they could have replaced it with uncontaminated blood. In pratice, that would have meant that $40,000,000 worth of blood was destroyed and expensive new blood screening technology would require to be purchased from the US. The Pasteur Institute had not, by then, developed its own screening method.

The Court heard that Dr Fevrier had urged that heat-treated alternatives be imported as soon as he became aware of the contamination. But his superiors did not act on his advice for another four months. He did not make their failure public.

A philosopher at the University of Paris, Rudolph de

Thuy, was asked for his opinion of the Court's decision in relation to Dr Fevrier and said:

'The heart of this matter is that Professor Fevrier failed a test but, it should be acknowledged, it was a test that most of us are never faced with. When he recognised a life-threatening danger, he took some steps to avert it but did not do everything in his power to do so. Of course, he did not create that life-threatening danger. No one did. Nonetheless, it is incontestable that had he protested publicly, lives might have been saved. Instead he confined himself to informing his superiors and was passive in the face of their subsequent inaction. It is conceivable that he thought they knew better. How many of us might have done the same? If a survey had been taken and the majority, thinking of their jobs, mortgages, children's school fees, etc., admitted that they would have done as he did, he is, plainly, being held to an unrealistically high standard and that is unjust. Supermen are supermen because they are exceptional. He should not be judged against that standard and the law should not require it.'

Alexander,

An old friend in Paris sent me this. Let us hope we are not to be judged as supermen (or women)!

Eileen

I would rather die today than end up in Saughton Prison. But France, French justice, is not so different from here. Age did not save Fevrier, why should it save me? Every day, I become less able to defend myself. I am sleeping little and the reports from my spies in the Inquiry are of little comfort. Yesterday, Tam Fenton had to walk into the place past a crowd of elbowing, placard-bearing protestors. He had an egg thrown at him and abuse yelled in his ear. Little do they know that the minute he learnt in the Netherlands that dry heat-treatment inactivated the virus, leaving the clotting product intact, he turned on a sixpence, heat-treated the lot and had the unheated stuff recalled. If the stuff hadn't worked and bleeds had occurred, he would have carried the can and been universally reviled. Lives were saved by him. He is, in fact, a superman.

Jean is off, taking little Garry to the dentist.

I heard today that the chap in charge of the north, whose name I cannot remember, is dead. Lucky fellow. He'd been in a home in Dalkeith for the last five years. I thought he was fully *compos mentis* but his obituary suggests otherwise. Eileen, who is to speak on two topics, phoned and warned me to look out for Lord Goodhart's interjected questions. She says he's a bit like Prof. Redland, quick but not as quick as he imagines. I am, she advises, to take my time, breathe, assemble my thoughts and proceed at a slow pace, my pace. He, she warns, will interrupt, huff and puff, and sometimes, out of devilment, lob a grenade. I must expect this.

Irma tells me she is being pursued by the Social

Security people and needs about £400 to ward them off. If she doesn't get it by Wednesday, she may lose her house. She told me this in the kitchen whilst failing to take the crusts off my sandwiches. Am I to help her? She's got one of her 'Grandkids' living with her at the moment, takes her to school. She didn't ask me for the money but, perhaps, she expected me to offer it? Should I? On the other hand, she told me off, good and proper, for sending money to all the various charities that now shower me with demands for money. I do not know what to do, am assaulted on all sides.

I read the entry she put in my care plan, or whatever the thing is called:

'Mr A was a little muddled tonight. Soup and sandwiches as normal.'

Soup? Where is my soup, I'd like to know!

11th May 2014

Without even seeing it, Eileen declined the offer of my sgian-dubh (on Bridget's part also). Irma might well be glad of the box of my Granny's seconds of assorted napery but said she needs to check with her husband first.

14th May 2014

Mr Irma, apparently, says no to the napery as it may be a Trojan horse for moths. The taxi man comforted me on the way back from the Eye Hospital by assuring me that I'd probably die before my glaucoma 'kicked in'. His wife, a fellow-sufferer, has eyelashes like Bambi from the drops.

As tomorrow is my first day at the Inquisition, once in

bed I looked over the timeline I prepared but could not recognise my own abbreviations, my own shorthand. Who is ACC? Have I correspondence from them?

15th May 2014
2 a.m.

Sleep is impossible. I laid out my clothes and looked over another sheaf of old notes. Talking to myself, I felt my mouth dry. I cannot take any more notes as, if I do, I become too agitated, my tremor becomes unmanageable. How can I explain what it felt like to be confronted with a completely new disease, spreading, picking off our patients? Assumptions were made, theories postulated, knowledge came slowly, mistakes were made. But always, always our motives were good.

Day 1 is over. By 2 p.m. I was so exhausted I kept finding I couldn't get the right word, hesitated, stuttered, made a fool of myself. Trying to tell them about the limits to the supplies of the safe treatment, cryoprecipitate, my mind went blank. Now, I can hardly see to type. It was largely formal stuff and I can't find the card telling me how to 'cut and paste' it. Jean has left the place like a new pin and, yesterday, must have put cream lilies in a vase in the drawing room for me. What a sweetie, she must have spent her own money on them. It's difficult. Lilies always remind me of funerals, last forever and I don't like having them in my house. A beef stroganoff was in my fridge.

Desperate to clear my mind, I hazarded a little shuffle towards the loch. Without Lucky to pull along, or sit down and become immoveable, I enjoyed my outing though there was a high wind. Back at my door, I had an overpowering feeling that someone was waiting in the shadows. I pretended not to see, looked away, locked my door behind me and put on the chain. Later, as I was on my way to bed, I heard the chain rattle.

I tried to haul myself upstairs to my old bedroom, using the banisters, but I had to give up at the first landing, descended the stairs on my bottom. I hate sleeping downstairs, I hate that little bed and I am afraid. I have no alarm, no shutters, windows break. I will not sleep.

16th May 2014

I was sick in the middle of last night and Jean phoned the Inquiry to explain my predicament. I'm to go tomorrow. When she was about to brush my hair, we found that my silver hairbrushes had left the premises. I bet Rough Andrea is at the bottom of it. At least twice I have found strands of her copper-coloured hairs in the bristles. Has she also taken my new post-it notes?

Twice, when I woke in the afternoon, I saw the same man outside my window. Once, he was looking in at me, his seamed face pressed hard against the pane. Jean says it's a trick of the light or somebody lost or something. But it isn't.

17th May 2014

My excretory system, once my obedient servant, has become

my master. All day as I was giving evidence it reminded me of my position, subjugating me, humbling me with a series of intermittent rumbles which the stenographer may have difficulty transcribing. I am reduced to a small child.

Lord Goodhart is, indeed, like Prof. Redland, only worse. We circled round and round Haemophilia B and Christmas disease and I still am not sure that he realises that they are the same condition. He and his Medical Assessor sit side by side at a desk; two small, round men like Tweedledum and Tweedledee. If one yawns the other follows suit and sometimes they nod together in unison, like a single two-headed creature.

I am only going to 'cut and paste' the bit of the transcript that I need to remind myself of. Copy onto a word document.

TRANSCRIPT

MISS POLSON: We have heard from other witnesses, Professor, that the absence of the clotting factor, known as Factor VIII, in the blood of those with haemophilia was, from the '70s onwards in Scotland, remedied by providing them with concentrates of Factor VIII?

WITNESS: Yes.

MISS POLSON: And those concentrates were administered by injection?

WITNESS: Yes, usually by the patient, that was the great advantage of this treatment. It was so easily done . . . so, er . . . effective, that for those with severe haemophilia prophylactic treatment was possible . . . then episodes of bleeding could be actually prevented.

MISS POLSON: Am I right in thinking that the factor concentrates were manufactured from large pools of blood donations?

WITNESS: Yes.

MISS POLSON: Now, at that time, these concentrates were manufactured in Scotland and in the USA, amongst other places?

WITNESS: Yes.

Miss Polson: Professor, can you tell me, firstly, a little about the commercial concentrates imported from the USA in the '70s and '80s?

WITNESS: Sorry, what did you say?

Miss Polson repeats the question.

WITNESS: I tried to ensure that my patients did not use them.

MISS POLSON: Why was that?

WITNESS: They were not safe.

MISS POLSON: What was unsafe about them?

WITNESS: Well, you see . . . unlike in America . . . our blood donation system is one based on the voluntary principle. I think most people in the UK are . . . pleased, no, er, glad, no . . . I know, proud of our system and rightfully so. No one who donates blood here expects any monetary reward, they donate because they believe they should donate. I'm sorry, could I have a glass of water, I'm losing my voice?

MISS POLSON: Of course.

(A glass of water is given to the witness)

WITNESS: Where was I . . . could it be read back to me?

Stenographer: You were saying 'they donate because they believe they should donate . . .'

WITNESS: Exactly. Sometimes they do it because they have themselves benefitted from the system, sometimes because a . . . lover, no, a loved one has done so. Sometimes, with a view to the future, and sometimes it's a purely . . . free . . . altruistic act. Those who donate on such a basis are likely to be good people, good citizens and their blood is likely to be safer from a micro . . . micro . . . microbiological point of view. Any products made from our domestic supply were therefore likely to be safer.

MISS POLSON: what was the problem with the commercial products imported from the USA?

WITNESS: What wasn't?

MISS POLSON: Could you, perhaps, elaborate?

WITNESS: There, money changed hands. The blood used to make the American, commercial stuff, the concentrates, was bought from people who tended to need the money very badly, the men who inhabit the, what's the expression . . . down and out places, you know . . . skid rows, that's it, of all of America's big cities. Don ation Centres tended to be in areas with bars, sex shops, peep-shows, lowdown areas frequented by alcoholics, drug addicts, the unemployed and down-and-outs . . . the low-downs.

MISS POLSON: And what is the significance of that?

WITNESS: The significance? Oh, right. Of course. Bought blood carries a higher risk of contamination. Studies, I can't remember which, suggest a risk six to seven times greater than donated blood. Blood was sold by those who needed the money, hence the US expression . . . er . . . what was it? Oh, yes. 'Ooze for booze'. Not healthy people – people with hepatitis, AIDS . . . desperate, poor unemployable people.

MISS POLSON: Were the US and also the UK concentrates both manufactured with pooled donated blood?

Witness: Mmm. Thousands of donations were pooled to make the product, in both countries. But there was, obviously, no mixing of the US and the Scottish blood. If you use a concentration technique to c-c-c-concentrate the required factor . . . it also concentrates the virus. You see, the larger the pool, the larger the risk of infection from the products.

MISS POLSON: Were the concentrates you prescribed for your patients in Scotland in the late '70s and early 80s made exclusively from pooled Scottish blood donations?

WITNESS: Sorry, I didn't catch your question.

MISS POLSON: (repeats the question)

WITNESS: The Scottish domestic product?

MISS POLSON: Yes.

WITNESS: Yes, for my patients, yes. Very largely, certainly.

MISS POLSON: How many donations were pooled, in that period, for the making of the concentrate?

WITNESS: In Scotland? For our product? I cannot say exactly, three, four thousand or so. I am not sure . . . I'm not sure I know that, accurately I mean, that I'm competent to answer that one?

MISS POLSON: is that a question more properly put to those responsible for the production of the Scottish product?

WITNESS: Yes, them. Definitely them.

MISS POLSON: We have heard from others, that in December 1984 all the Scottish concentrates, Factor VIII, were heat-treated in order to inactivate the AIDS virus in the product?

WITNESS: Yes.

MISS POLSON: So, up until December 1984, the use of the concentrates you were prescribing for your patients was known to carry the risk of transmitting the AIDS virus?

WITNESS: I'm sorry, what . . . What are you suggesting, that I knew . . . ?

LORD GOODHART: Four o'clock, ladies and gentlemen. This opens up a new, important and contentious chapter, so I think we'll start it tomorrow. We will resume at ten o'clock sharp tomorrow morning.

Thinking, far less speaking, exhausts me. By the end of

the session, keeping my words in order in front of all those people is almost beyond me. How can I go on another day? Two weeks of this will finish me off.

I do not want to go back to that place. Trying to stiffen my resolve, I reminded myself about another of my forebears, General Sir Donald Anstruther.

'At the storming of Ahmednagar his gallantry was sufficiently conspicuous for him to be put on Wellington's staff, becoming the great man's ADC by 1807. Three horses were killed under him in battle and by 1815 he was a Colonel, fighting with the Duke at Quatre Bras and at Waterloo. He became a full General and by 1833 was Governor of New South Wales.'

That's what the book says. His blood runs through my veins. My Grandad had his sword: today it hangs, together with two others, in my hallway.

No horses have been killed under me. But this is my Waterloo, and I mustn't fail my family. I mustn't run away. It feels more like my court martial. But soldiers try soldiers because only they understand what may happen in the heat of battle. For me, lawyers are trying doctors. Have they the imagination to put themselves in our places? I doubt anyone could. A brand-new disease, a potential epidemic, people ill, then people dying, amongst them my patients, and no one, no one, knew why. Life and death decisions, and all in the dark.

Two black puddings, cold, for my supper. Has Jean returned my sister Isabel's letters? I thought we had done them, that they were in date-order already?

At about 7 p.m. I looked in the fridge and saw I had no milk. I managed to shuffle to the newsagent with my stick, and on my return journey, someone followed me. I heard their footsteps behind me. I turned around but they must have ducked into an alley. Someone was there, though, and in my fear I thought my heart might break through my ribs, beating so hard. Someone is trying to scare me, or worse. Jean does not believe me.

18th May 2014

TRANSCRIPT

MISS POLSON: Yesterday, I asked you if you contiued treating your patients with unsafe non-heat-treated Scottish concentrates up until the end of 1984, but we did not get your answer. Could you tell us today?

WITNESS: Well, I began treatment with heat-treated products in about December 1984, as soon as . . . erm . . . as soon as . . . as soon as they became . . . were available . . . to us. The heat kills the virus . . . but the blood-clotting property remains.

MISS POLSON: So, is that a yes?

WITNESS: Until December 1984 I . . . er . . . er . . . treated with non-heat-treated Scottish products, yes. That's all we had.

MISS POLSON: You would agree with me,

Professor, that it has been known, since at least around the middle of the last century, that blood transfusions could transmit infection via blood-borne viruses?

WITNESS: Yes.

MISS POLSON: Similarly, that products made from that donated blood could transmit infection via blood-borne viruses?

WITNESS: Yes, Hepatitis B, for example. Unfortunately, almost all my patients were infected with it.

MISS POLSON: Indeed. Now, can you tell me at what approximate date you became convinced that HIV/AIDS was a blood-borne virus?

WITNESS: It was a gradual process . . . it happened . . . At this distance in time I can't say it was this day or that day, pin it down like that. I just can't say . . . now, it's all so long ago . . . I don't have a date . . . in that way. Late 1984, perhaps.

MISS POLSON: Am I correct in understanding that the results of the study that you carried out on your haemophilia patients in 1983 showed that some of them were exhibiting immune abnormalities similar to those reported earlier in some homosexuals, haemophiliacs and IV drug-users in America who later developed AIDS?

WITNESS: Yes, I think so. Yes.

MISS POLSON: So, such immune abnormalities appeared to be associated with infection with the virus?

WITNESS: Yes.

MISS POLSON: Is the incidence in homosexuals,

haemophiliacs and IV drug-users of blood-borne viruses, such as Hepatitis B, higher than in the general population?

WITNESS: Yes.

MISS POLSON: Did those abnormal 1983 results, plus that known higher incidence, not suggest to you that HIV/AIDS might be a blood-borne virus, before the end of 1984?

WITNESS: No, it is not as simple as that . . . not as simple.

MISS POLSON: Perhaps you could explain?

WITNESS: Yes, you see my haemophilia patients, including those with abnormal test results, were treated, exclusively, with the Scottish product.

MISS POLSON: Yes, I appreciate that, but what's the significance of that?

WITNESS: Well, you see . . . er . . . I took the view that as there were no known cases of AIDS in our own blood-donor population, the immunosuppression observed in my haemophiliacs must have resulted either from . . . er . . . the infusion of foreign proteins that they received every time they injected themselves with the concentrates, damage to their immune system caused by the foreign proteins, antigen overload . . . sorry, I've gone blank. Could the question and my answer be read back to me?

(Stenographer reads out question and answer.)

WITNESS: Yes, that's right . . . or some other wide-spread virus.

MISS POLSON: So, you, relying on the supposed

76

purity of the Scottish blood supply, concluded that the immune deficiencies you found in your patients must be caused by something other than AIDS-contaminated blood? They couldn't be infected by it because it wasn't infected, so the immune deficiencies had to be caused by something else?'

WITNESS: Yes... exactly.

MISS POLSON: And you were wrong?

WITNESS: Er, yes, that's right. I know that now... nowadays, yes.

MISS POLSON: But, let's think about any such reliance on the purity of the Scottish product. People travel from the USA to Scotland and vice versa, don't they, Professor? Even back in the late '70s, early '80s, 1981, 1982 and 1983, they did that, didn't they?

WITNESS: Yes, they did.

MISS POLSON: And homosexuals and intravenous drug addicts were to be found in Scotland in the late '70s, early 80s?

WITNESS: Yes, they were ... we've always had, I think, homosexuals and IV drug users in our population, I accept that.

MISS POLSON: American homosexuals might travel to Scotland and start relationships with Scottish homosexuals?

WITNESS: Yes, of course, but ...

MISS POLSON: An American IV drug user might travel here, end up sharing a needle with a Scottish IV user – or vice versa?

WITNESS: Yes, but . . .

MISS POLSON: Up until early 1984 blood was collected from Scottish prisoners, some incarcerated for their IV drug use, some homosexual?

WITNESS: Yes, but by 1983 . . .

MISS POLSON: Are you suggesting that . . .

LORD GOODHART: Miss Polson, please do not talk over, harry this witness. You must let him finish. In any event, we have reached the end of today's session and you can continue, if you wish, with this line tomorrow.

MISS POLSON: But this witness is no longer scheduled for tomorrow, we are going to have to inter-pose Dr Cairns as he's just heard he's got a date for his knee-replacement. Naturally, he cannot miss it. He's going to come tomorrow and for the next few days, week or whatever, as he won't be available the next week.

LORD GOODHART: Very well, then, the next scheduled day or whenever. It has been a long day for us all.

She is circling round me like a vulture over a dying beast.

20th May 2014

I am drained. Bridget phoned to say that Eileen has finished our second joint submission and should she bring it round. I cannot face it, so I said no, I would not need to see it as I had no doubt that Eileen would have done a first-class job. I no longer know where the first one has been filed.

My bowels are not working.

Something is wrong with me, peeing is painful as if I'm excreting acid and the stuff in the pan looked mahogany-coloured. When I have time, I must go to the surgery. Are my kidneys malfunctioning? I'll get Irma to get me a carton of milk until I see someone.

One shattering piece of news. Jean submitted her latest inventory in the cataloguing work that she has been doing for me, and appearing at No. 845 was the letter I kept from Roddy, described by her as 'Personal. Letter No. 845 (1958) from Roderick Gammell – love letter'. I will have put it in that pile for safe-keeping, God help me. From now on, it'll stay here, in my journal, safe from any other prying eyes.

NO. 845:
LETTER FROM RODERICK GAMMELL

12 Newton Street
Durham
13th March 1958

Alex

I am not prepared to go on any longer. I wrote those poems for you and you alone. You know that, knew it when first you read them.

I do love you.

As a scientist, you think truth is simple, easily discerned, subject to analysis and all very black and white, almost mathematical. I do not. It is not. I may, occasionally, boast, exaggerate or tell a downright lie but I still understand it in a way that you do not. How often have I said I love you? That is a truth, and one that I openly declare. I do not know if you love me or not. How could I? You have never said so, and I cannot go on not knowing. Is it fear of the police? Fear of what your family might think? Fear of yourself? Can you not face yourself, accept yourself for what you are? I bet there have been homosexual Anstruthers before, probably one or more of your distinguished Admirals or Generals. A pretty midshipman, perhaps? There, I have said the H word, pulled it out into the open. This is not a 'phase', take my word for it. If you were to marry a woman you would be doing her a severe wrong.

I should have told you about my period in jail. It all happened about four years ago, and, to be honest, when I was desperately lonely. I knew Wildeblood at Oxford, kept up with him after we both left. I think he and I were only prosecuted because of Lord Montagu's involvement. All we did, and it's all pretty innocent, was drink, dance and kiss. Montagu got twelve months, Peter got eighteen and I got eight. I was too ashamed to say anything to you about it, it still sounds so sordid, dirty (although it was not), but I'm sorry you found out about it from someone else. What I am not sorry about is that this has brought everything to a head; too much has been unspoken between us.

You should read Peter's book 'Against the Law'. It would make you think.

You are doing so well in medicine; continue working hard, you will be a consultant before you can say 'Bingo'. But, take it from someone older than you (ten years is longer than you think!), you will make an even better doctor if you accept yourself, understand that love is as fine, as sacred, between a man and a man as between a man and a woman. Humanity comes in many shapes and sizes, everyone's eyes are not blue, some people are left-handed. Some are tall, some are small . . . have I touched a nerve?

You are perfect.

And I love you. Meet me on Saturday at 8 p.m. at L'Aperitif in Frederick Street and we can have dinner and gawp at the naked mermaids on the walls? The odd merman too. If you love someone, it is as much of a lie not to answer them when they ask you if you love them as it is to answer 'No'. You turn away, never answer me.

Do you love me?

If I do not get a reply to this I will understand and not write again.

All my love,
Roderick

It was a phase, Roddy; there was a woman once or twice. But rarely after you, I must admit, love. Now, I am an old man, an old fool.

Has my Jean read it? Of course. How otherwise could she catalogue it as 'Personal, etc.' and not? I'm beginning to worry that she knows far too much about me, might black-mail me or, at least, expose me to the papers. 'Sell her story' to the *Sun*. 'Doc treating haemophiliacs during the Gay Plague was secretly Gay', or something. I know virtually nothing about her, she blew in off the streets and became a part of my life. All of that was a secret, NOBODY knew, not even Isabel. If the Bad Blood people learnt they would use it against me too, suggest I passed on AIDS? What will she think of me now? This is my private life. I do not understand these kind of people, I must be careful with her. A tad over-familiar, she kissed me on the cheek before she left yesterday. I froze. I ate most of the cake she baked for me, but it tasted dry, bitter. Food bores me.

No one knew.

I think I saw that same man outside my window again, with my own eyes. Jean poo-poos it but someone was there. Perhaps she is just trying to comfort me? Or, perhaps, she knows him? Does she think I have lost my mind, have delu-sions? Why is she pretending that she cannot see him? Have I lost my mind?

I wonder how Eileen will get on with Lord Goodhart. She is the epitome of grace under pressure, nothing ever seemed to discombobulate her. I rang her up on that dread-ful night, when I discovered that some of my haemophilia patients had tested positive for the virus. I was, I am sorry to say, panicking, appalled at the unbelievable news. Just thinking about it now, I can feel sweat running down my back. I will not sleep. I did not kill them, I did not give them that disease, no one meant this to happen. If I had my time again would I do things differently? No, because I would be as ignorant as I was first time round, make the same well-intentioned mistakes. I am not a God, I do see through a glass darkly, know only in part. Where is Jean?

22nd May 2014

Jean left a message to say she cannot come today as she's ill. How am I to manage? I tipped over a cardboard box of papers in my study and my knees are too stiff and sore for me to bend to pick them up. Were they in date-order?

A man from the council appeared, breathed garlic over me, saying 'Mr Anstruther, you're to be re-assessed.' Apparently, Rough Andrea has told the Office that I need more help. No more hand-grabbers, rails, commodes etc. for me, thank you very much. Now, a pair of new knees? I'd indent for them immediately. He sat next to me and filled in the form for me but gave up halfway, asking 'You alright, pal?', then told me he'd finish the rest in the office and I should ring NHS 24. Why? Do they have a cure for old age?

I am not his pal.

23rd May 2014

Jean did not come today so I rang her. A man answered and passed the receiver to her. She said she had a flu-like bug that she did not want to pass on to me. But I wonder.

Who was the man? She has no brothers, I know that. Irma told me that she lost her last job; that never came out at my interview! When I asked why, all Irma would say was that her employer no longer wanted her. Why? Maybe she tried to worm her way into his affections too. Maybe I am one of many.

I am to appear again at the Inquiry in six days' time. Rough Andrea scalded me with the shower last night. She said it was a malfunction, that the control dial did not respond but, despite my cries, she was slow to react, galumphing round the basin, and missing the dial first time. I am to fill in an 'Accident Book' for the Agency. I suppose it was an accident.

I saw what she wrote in my notes:

'Mr A got a scald. He turned the dial the wrong way.'

'He' did not turn the dial the wrong way. The next time the Agency seek my appraisal of their care-givers' services, I shall not be so reticent. My joints are aching and I have a pain in my side. An unknown GP came with my prescriptions, uninvited, to take my BP. I still have no Omeprazole.

He asked me my name (!), where I lived (!). What is this youth doing delivering drugs if he isn't sure of the recipients? I displayed my scald to him but he disregarded it, asking, casually, whether 'when the time comes' I wish CPR. No, I replied, 'when the time comes, I wish treatment for my scald'.

Last night, I dreamt again that I was being questioned. Miss Polson was snapping at me, I tried to speak but my words would not come out and I knew, knew that I was sunk. Lord Goodhart himself interrupted, and he, too, was getting angry with me, roaring at me, spitting his commands at me, to speak up, man, speak sense. My mouth would not work, I opened it but no words emerged. I think I have a temperature, I feel so ill, I must have one. I cannot go back, I will let them all down.

I dropped this journal and the jail cutting that Eileen sent flew out and I read it again. I am not going to go to prison. I saw them in that place, bled the prisoners, listened to their lewd chat. I would rather die. My obituary will not relate that my final address was Saughton: Anstruther of Saughton. It will not.

25th May 2014

To my dismay I was asked to fill in at the Inquiry, on an emergency basis, today, as Dr Cairns was in a road-traffic accident last night. He is, D.V., to return to the Inquiry tomorrow.

MISS POLSON: Very good of you to come today, Professor, and rather than returning to the topic we were discussing on the last occasion you were with us, I'd like to interject another one, for the moment, as Dr Cairns has been giving us the benefit of his evidence on it. The topic is 'Information Given to Patients and Patient Consents'.

WITNESS: I see, I see. Right, 'Information Given to Patients . . . and Consents'.

MISS POLSON: Am I correct in understanding

that you treated the witness, whom we are calling Dennis, from the age of about three onwards for haemophilia?

WITNESS: Yes, I treated Pat . . . er, Dennis. If that's what we're calling him.

MISS POLSON: I understand that Dennis was amongst those of your patients who contracted the AIDS virus as a result of the treatment he received with Scottish Factor VIII?

WITNESS: Dennis was amongst that group, the . . . er . . . cohort of my patients infected with the AIDS virus, yes. He had been treated exclusively with Factor VIII made from Scottish blood . . . yes, exclusively Scottish blood.

MISS POLSON: Can you tell us how you became aware that some of your patients, including Dennis, had become infected?

WITNESS: I can, yes. I can. Now let me think . . . Yes. The minute I became aware that an antibody test had been developed, I, like the rest of my colleagues, sent off some blood samples that we had stored in the deep freeze in the department . . . sent them off, you know, to be examined . . . no, tested. They were tested.

MISS POLSON: When was that?

WITNESS: Mmm. Some point about late autumn 1984, I'd think. From memory.

MISS POLSON: Tell me this. Were the patients whose blood was tested informed, pre-testing, that their blood was to be used in such a test?

WITNESS: No, no. You see, periodically, in accordance with good practice, we took blood for virological testing and clotting . . . ass . . . ass . . . assays, and kept it in the deep freeze in the department. The blood sent had been taken previously . . . earlier, if you will . . . for those purposes. So we won't have told them, got their consent. When the blood was taken we had no idea when testing would even become available. D'you see? No, we won't have told them or let them know, not then. We couldn't . . . didn't know about the existence of that kind of testing then.

MISS POLSON: But you could have asked them prior to testing, albeit after you'd taken the blood?

WITNESS: Mmm. No one did that then . . . none of my colleagues, I'm sure no one did that then.

MISS POLSON: Something else I want to ask you about. When you learnt that Dennis, amongst others, had the AIDS virus, I assume that you informed them all, including him, of that positive result?

WITNESS: No. No, I didn't.

MISS POLSON: No? Surely, if anyone had a right to know, he had a right to know?

WITNESS: It is not as . . . s . . . s . . . simple as that. There was no treatment at the time, remember? People were dying. It was a 'deadly disease'. Anyone who had AIDS was stigmatised, jobs lost, accommodation lost, mortgages refused . . . er . . . schools refusing pupils . . . some people, some people just did not want to know . . . some surgeons refused to operate, those with the virus were subject to abuse, discrimination, dentists wouldn't touch their mouths . . . things were utterly different from nowadays. Like I said, some people . . . actually, positively, didn't want to know.

MISS POLSON: So, what did you do?

WITNESS: I remember that . . . yes. I wrote to all my patients, every one, every one, telling them that there was an apparent AIDS problem in the Scottish haemophilia population . . . yes, and that a test for the antibody, the body's reaction to exposure to the virus, now existed. I invited them to come to the department . . . my department . . . to give a new sample . . . then a test could be carried out with their consent, you see. When they came I would tell them I already had some results and ask them if they would like to know whether they had already been tested, and if so, the result.

MISS POLSON: How did they respond?

WITNESS: How did they respond? Well, well, some immediately wanted to know if they'd been tested and to get their results; some simply did not want to know. Some refused then but came back a bit later. We offered counselling, Miss Hepburn helped . . . but, as I say, we had no cure, no treatment. It was a death sentence.

MISS POLSON: Turning back to Dennis?

WITNESS: Yes.

MISS POLSON: Did Dennis want to know?

WITNESS: No, Dennis did not want to know. I remember that . . . remember that vividly.

MISS POLSON: So, you just went along with that, his wishes, and did not tell him?

WITNESS: He was my patient, he was *compos*

mentis . . . it was his decision. I did not blame him, he was not alone in making that decision. It was not my decision to make. I could not force him, I could not shut him in a room . . .

LORD GOODHART: Take your time, Professor.

WITNESS: Thank you, yes. I will. I couldn't shut him in a room, lock the door. I gave him the choice, what more could I do? He decided he didn't want to know.

MISS POLSON: But did it not cross your mind, Professor, that the patients might need to know in order to ensure that they did not pass the infection on to others? As you are aware, Dennis passed the infection on to his wife . . .'

WITNESS: I am aware and regret that result. But . . . but . . . I, no, we did our utmost, consistent with respect for the autonomy . . . yes, the autonomy of the patient. We told them all, impressed upon them all, said they must be very careful with blood spillages and sex. We told them that they must live their lives AS IF (Witness's emphasis) a diagnosis of AIDS had been given to them, as if they were positive . . . that way they would keep others safe. Safe, safe as houses, if you like. Well, you know what I mean.

MISS POLSON: I see. But, at one stage, in about the beginning of 1987, you took it upon yourself to inform Dennis of his diagnosis . . . whether he wanted to know or not. Given what you have already told us, perhaps, you can explain why you took that decision at that time? Dennis' wife had been found positive for the virus, as I'm sure you are aware, in 1985. It was too late for her.

WITNESS: I can explain . . . I can explain.

MISS POLSON: Then please do, Professor.

WITNESS: Dennis was seen by us throughout '84, '85 and '86. Yes, the mid-'80s as I . . . think, no, recall. It'll all be in the records, won't it? Anyway, every time he came to us . . . for routine monitoring, tests and so on, we reminded him that he might want to know his results . . . but he was adamant, adamant, that he did not want to know. I offered to visit him at home. Lalla, Dr Munro, in the department tried to persuade him. By the end of '85 . . . no, not '85, it was '86 . . . we were beginning to treat with Zidovudine, there was some prophylaxis against pneumocystis. Pentamidine had become available. He was clearly symptomatic, you know, things were happening to him . . . distressing things as I recall. So, I took it upon myself . . . I decided, really, to tell him then because there was, at last, treatment. We had something to offer, to help him . . .

MISS POLSON: What was his reaction to the news?

WITNESS: (sighs) He was angry, very angry, with me.

MISS POLSON: Why?

WITNESS: I have never really understood that. Although every time we saw him we tried to persuade him to ask, he did not seem to have worked out that there might have been a reason for that, an obvious reason for that. An obvious reason for that . . . obvious to anyone surely? Why else would we have been so pressing, you understand? But he seemed genuinely surprised, amazed even. To be completely honest, I was startled by his reaction . . . because . . . because . . . I thought, at some level, he must have known he had it.

MISS POLSON: He was in denial?

WITNESS: I suppose he was.

(Call from Public Benches: Liar! Liar!)

LORD GOODHART: Quiet, please.

MISS POLSON: Even if Dennis did not want to know, could you not have warned his wife?

WITNESS: Patient confidentiality forbids it, that's fundamental for all of us . . . it had to be up to him, it was up to him.

MISS POLSON: One further matter, Professor. But before that, would another glass of water be helpful? You seem to be becoming increasingly hoarse.

WITNESS: Thank you.

MISS POLSON: If you are feeling too tired or ill, Professor . . .

WITNESS: I will tell you.

MISS POLSON: What I want to know is why, prior to late autumn 1984, you did not warn your patients about the risk they might be being exposed to from possible contamination of the Scottish blood supply, resulting in the possible contamination of the products made from it, including the Factor VIII used by them?

WITNESS: I'm sorry, what . . .

MISS POLSON: A clumsy question, my fault. I'll

try and reformulate. Why did you not warn those of your patients taking Factor VIII of the risk to them posed by it until late autumn 1984?

WITNESS: Yes, I see. Well, in the beginning, we did not know what level of risk, if any, our patients were being exposed to. We could not . . . what's the word? Er . . . er . . . qualify, no, quantify it. As time went on we still didn't know what to do. Should we wait for the statistics to . . . to . . . to enlighten us to the level of risk or should we tell the patients about the risk, regardless of the prob-ability of infection, simply because the consequences of infection might be so . . . dreadful . . . so great? By late 1983, no, late '84, we knew the likely infective agent, we knew it had been found in a number of Scottish patients. Patients who had only used the Scottish product. That's when we started discussing the risk . . . discussing it, discussing it with the patients. Is that clear?

MISS POLSON: Very, thank you, but were there no substitutes that you could have offered them?

WITNESS: Not really.

MISS POLSON: Why not?

WITNESS: Mmm. You need to understand, the use of Factor VIII revolutionised patients' lives, their lives became all but . . . n . . . normal. In 1960, pre-Factor VIII, with severe haemophilia, the life expectancy was less than twenty years. That's why the Haemophilia Society, the haemophiliacs' own society, were so desperate . . . yes, so desperate . . . to ensure that American commercial Factor VIII continued to be imported into England. Scotland, you understand, was self-sufficient in its home-grown product, England was not. To cope with the demand . . . England had to import from America . . . from commercial companies, buyers of blood.

MISS POLSON: Shouldn't you, nonetheless, have erred on the side of caution?

WITNESS: That's easy to say now. Easy, easy, with hindsight. But if I'd warned, before . . . before we really knew about the size, the gravity, of the risk, gave a false alarm, I'd be standing here now trying to explain why my false alarm had resulted in my patients' disability, severe disability, aneurysms, blindness or death, when no risk, in fact, existed. All I can tell you, again, is that I did my best.

LORD GOODHART: As I said, Professor, just take your time. Apart from anything else, if it all comes out in a torrent, in a gabble, it's very difficult for the stenographer.

WITNESS: I'll try.

MISS POLSON: If you had told them what you knew, however limited it was, when you knew it, it would have been their choice?

WITNESS: Yes.

MISS POLSON: Should it have been their choice?

WITNESS: Then, no. We didn't think so. Now, yes, indubitably, yes. Thinking, attitudes, mores . . . change, alter, evolve over time . . . once animals were hanged for crimes, bears baited, little children sent up chimneys and right-thinking people slept easy in their beds at night.

MISS POLSON: Were there any ethical guidelines covering the situation in which you found yourself?

93

WITNESS: None, the situation was unprecedented. No one, no one anywhere, advised us what to do, there was no guidance from on high, from the health department, government or something. As I said, all, each of us could do, was our best. Our best . . . I tried, did do my best.

MISS POLSON: If I was to . . .

LORD GOODHART: I think this witness has probably had enough questions for today, Miss Polson, don't you? He's clearly flagging, struggling a bit now. And as one elderly man to another, I sympathise with the Professor. He has, I can see, quite run out of energy and we may need his services again. I think we'll either end today's proceedings with his evidence or fit in a short witness, if anyone is available?

MISS POLSON: No one is available and we'll be continuing with Dr Cairns tomorrow, unless he's being detained in hospital.

LORD GOODHART: Very good, Miss Polson. When is Professor Anstruther to return?

MISS POLSON: On 1st June.

I am a rag. I cannot keep things together much longer.

26th May 2014

No Jean. Five days to go. Jimmy Ward phoned to pass on that he'd seen Gavin Threadneedle at the New Club, describing him as 'A husk in a wheelchair'. When we were both housemen at the Infirmary, we used to run along those long, cold corridors at full pelt, jumping up to touch the bare lightbulbs out of sheer *joie de vivre*. His legs were like springs then.

I am a husk, too. I cannot go back.

27th May 2014

No Jean. I rang and a man answered so I put the phone down. Four days to go. How does Garry get to school, if she is ill? Surely he's too small to go on his own?

28th May 2014

[CUTTING FROM THE *SCOTSMAN*,
DATED 25TH MAY 2014,
with handwritten note by 'Eileen']

THE BLOODY LIE

'The Bloody Lie' by Una Sassoon sets out to expose the secrets of the 'Tainted Blood' scandal. It is, of course, more than up to the moment, anticipating the results of the Judicial Inquiry which continues its investigation into that very matter. The play is built around a series of formalised conversations and recorded interviews between a couple of old physicians. It appears to be set in a disused warehouse, but it could be an old hospital or almost any other deserted building. Periodically, a collection of 'ghosts' wander between them, touching their ears, blowing on the tops of their heads and being flicked away like flies. The costumes in this production seem to have come from the sale rack at Primark or, possibly, Nylons R Us. Some of the cast crackle and spark, literally, but not in a good way.

Bizarrely, the director, Jan Gough, has opted for so-called gender-blind casting. In particular, all the haemophiliacs are played by women or girls. This is, apparently, 'to emphasise the powerlessness of the patient'. What it actually emphasises is the ineptitude of the director.

To compound matters further, Ms Sassoon has, unfortunately, chosen to subordinate her characters, or any character development, to the use of quasi-ritualised dialogue to ensure that her point is not missed by the audience. Frankly one might as easily miss a punch on the nose. As a result, the evening is little more than an extended propaganda session, but at a theatre ticket price. On the night I attended the audience reacted, initially, with gasps of disbelief and, as the evening progressed, bouts of uneasy laughter.

An additional shortcoming of this play is the characterisation of the two main protagonists, Drs Crail and Barbour. The former is written to personify the Pantomime Villain, cold and unfeeling, rubbing his hands, concerned with nothing but his own reputation and the needs of his dog 'Lucky'. Dr Crippen would be a more sympathetic medical man. What on earth attracted Luke Sinclair to play this wooden, unconvincingly written part? The unfortunate Isla Drew has similar difficulties with her role as Dr Elizabeth Barbour. She, too, has to portray a character apparently entirely lacking in humanity, and while through her expressions, mannerisms and tone of voice she valiantly endeavors to bestow some human feeling upon her part, she fails. Dame Judy herself would, I suspect, be unable to do a better job, so leaden is the writing.

The performances of most of the supporting cast, playing bemused nurses, patients or the dumbstruck parents of the patients, are, like their costumes, patchy. Emma Derby, after her marvellous performance as Goneril in Kearn's Lear last month, struggled valiantly but deserved better fare. Daniela McGowan and Rita Ross sank without a trace and seemed only too eager to scuttle off the stage. Francis Tuttaford appeared to have concluded that his fellow actors were deaf and spent his time shouting at them like a drill sergeant at Pirbright. The ghosts, perhaps unsurprisingly, made only the faintest impression, except for eleven-year-old Sukie Haden's performance as ghost Peter, patient number 3.

> 'The gift you gave to save my life
> Ended it as could a knife,
> Tainted blood pumped in my arm
> Made a lie of Do No Harm.'

Ms Sassoon wrote 'The Dog's Day Out' which I saw and much enjoyed when it was performed at the Traverse last year. It was witty, perceptive and original. As I predicted, it quickly moved on to the West End. In contrast, this play lacks that trio of qualities and others beside. I do not know why the Albion was prepared to put on this lacklustre piece and I very much doubt that it will find a place in the Official Festival this summer. It makes MacDonald's 'Factor 9', a play concerned with similar subject matter, in comparison seem Pinteresque in its subtlety. In her interview in the *Evening News* Ms Sassoon described her play as 'nuanced and non-judgemental'. Unfortunately, that is a Bloody Lie if ever there was one.

Dear Alexander

I hope you are enjoying a good rest before you are required to attend the Inquiry again. I saw this play advertised and, unable to face it myself after sitting through that 'Factor 9' play, (the one the 'Tainted Blood' members helped with) I asked Bridget if she would mind going. Unselfishly, she went and her verdict was very similar to that of the *Scotsman*'s critic. I don't know anything about the playwright but I noted that her 'technical advisor' was Ian Shade, one of my patients, now suffering from AIDS. Your patient, Gordon Janssen, was also so described.

Take care of yourself my old friend, I thought you looked

exhausted the last time I saw you. I'll phone in the next few days about the paper on life expectancy.

Best wishes
Eileen

PS Bridget sends her good wishes.

Words fail me.

29th May 2014

Three days. No Jean and I miss her bright presence so. Irma says that she saw her up and about in Stockbridge, but, obviously, she does not consider herself well enough to come here to me. She can't need the money. I am still not well and the chicken soup that I took from my deep freeze, bought by her, has lumps. I should be revising, checking the dates of decisions, reasons and so on but I can't. How did that playwright know about Lucky? Did Jean tell them, could she be feeding information to people like Ian Shade or Gordon or that Sassoon woman directly? For all I know about her, she may have been helping the Bad Blood people too? But why should she hate me? I am afraid of her and I hope she does not come back. Maybe they pay her? That man that she knows was at my window again, I shut the curtains but I could hear him moving about on the gravel outside my front door.

I went into the hall and stood stock-still beside it and I could hear him through the panelled wood perfectly.

He seemed to be sniffing it, like a dog, then he tried a key in the lock. I froze. I heard him turn it, and leant my shoulder against the door, frantic that he should not get in. I heard him curse, try again and then thump the door. I went back to bed, chittering with fear. My phone did not work. In the morning, again, you could have wrung my sheets out. I am cold. No one changed them and they are clammy yet.

30th May 2014

Two days to go. No Jean. Have I even got her telephone number anymore? Nowhere is quiet, nowhere is safe.

31st May 2014

One day to go. Thank God, Jean is coming tonight. Looked in the paper and saw an interview with Gaynor Todd. She said that the doctors killed her boy and mentioned me and Ken by name.

SECOND NARRATIVE *by*
ANTHONY SPARROW

Now it's my voice alone you will hear, because Professor Anstruther's has fallen silent. I was disappointed to lose his, I must admit. I had grown to like the old fellow's company, and my interest in him and concern for his fate had increased since I had come to understand, or thought I did, the man. As I mentioned earlier, I suspect mine were the first eyes to feast upon the journal since the black blots spattered throughout it had dried. In so far as it is dated, it ends upon the 31st of May 2014. There are another couple of pages of script in the middle of the journal, undated, but the writing is all over the place and I found his spidery hand micrographic and impossible to decipher. I tried hard, believe me, acquiring a 'Magik' magnifying glass ('See like a teenager!') from one of those mags majoring in incontinence pads, de-luxe walking frames and other goodies enjoyed by the elderly, and, to my chagrin, sent to me unsolicited.

Now, much of what I touched amongst his possessions had acquired Meaning. A cache of lavender bags, one of which had been used as a cushion for his key ceremony, his University tie, his elusive watch. Fingering his old-fashioned stethoscope, I could visualise it dangling low on his sunken chest. His possessions were no longer simply things. I would like to say that, as a rule, I do not clear for my nearest and dearest. But those would be empty words; like him, I have no nearest and dearest. In the early days, knowing that a murder had taken place in Anstruther's abode gave the task, to my, possibly warped, sensibilities, a sort of ghoulish glamour. Having heard the dead man's voice, it now troubled me and made my task morose, if not ghoulish, plain and simple. So many questions remained unanswered in my mind. Why had his attitude to his factotum changed as he got to know her? Who was haunting him, prowling around the house, and why? What was Jean Whitadder's attitude to her employer?

Whilst I was manhandling a glass case containing a couple of stuffed red squirrels staring, in glassy-eyed terror, at a stoat, an entomological scholar of my acquaintance, Dr Ford-Maxwell, phoned to say, if I acted fast, I might be able to scoop up the contents of a library. It belonged to a spinster lady of considerable means in Selkirk.

'There are some I want, only two or three . . .' he begged, 'for the tip off?'

'My, my,' I replied.

'One?'

A beau had entered her life, fond of billiards, and 'clearance' was required. The bookcases and their contents were to be removed, sacrificed to the couples' desire to pot blacks, or whatever, in their new domestic bliss. I turned the opportunity down.

'*Nein danke, Oswald, mein freund,*' I said 'No can do.'

Why? Because it was urgent, because my work in

Anstruther's house would be interrupted, and I had a new obsession. All I wanted to do, yearned to do, was to find out exactly what happened to the man, complete my self-appointed task. In some strange, illogical way I felt that I had heard his voice as no one else had, that he was calling me. Me, personally. I had to act on it. God knows, I should tremble if I knew no one else could save me but me. I would not like to be my own knight in shining armour; a charger bald from alopecia, lance like a corkscrew and rust-speckled visor jammed shut. But he had no one else.

Police? Please! Having been manhandled by them, courtesy of an aggrieved Mancunian client who assured them I was a 'fence', I would no more rely on their conclusions than on those of a lobotomised horse. In fact, on mature reflection, I'd favour empty-headed Dobbin's yeas or neighs. The journal was mine and for my eyes alone. I'd follow in their over-large footsteps but, if the fancy took me, take the path untrodden.

One of the few advantages that I do possess is that I know people. You can hardly reach my own considerably advanced age without doing so. Still, credit where credit is due. It is my Genius. Like a fat spider, I preside over a complex web and, periodically, flies collide with my sticky threads, become trapped in my silk. Insatiable bibliophiles routinely buzz and wriggle in them, though they rarely break free. But I am after their money, not their lives. I sympathise with these people, understand them. They are my tribe. In 2014 Stephen Bone killed Archie Duncan in order to get his hands on one of the first illustrated editions of Mary Shelley's *Frankenstein*. I was on sherry terms with both, but, personally, I draw the line at murder.

To explain the nature of our relationship properly, let me use a different, perhaps more apt metaphor; bibliophilia is a form of possession, an addiction, a positively pathological desire for books. Myself, I am both user and dealer. I became dependent at a tender age; grew high on the scent of the vellum, not the glue. I am not normal, no longer feel the need to even pretend to be. In my teens, sex never came into it, left me quite cold. Whereas I dream, literally dream, of Vesalius's *De Corporis Fabrica Libri Septum*. Other men may long to caress the curves of a buxom blonde, a svelte brunette. Me? I would die happy with my arms around Combe's *Anatomical Study of the Regions of the Head*. Odd, you might think (if not voice), creepy even. We book addicts are hidden but we are Legion.

Fiddle dee dee.

Now, my own true love, as you may have guessed, is phrenology. For the uninitiated, it is a quasi-medical (some would say, pseudo-medical) discipline concerned with the appearance of the skull as an indicator of the nature of the mind contained therein. Phrenologists believed that the brain was the organ of the mind, and that certain brain areas had specific, localised functions. Accordingly, they would examine a patient's skull for enlargements or indentations likely to be eloquent of character. Like Elias Ashmole (a keen follower of phrenology), of Ashmolean Library fame, my 'area of acquisitiveness' is exceptionally well-developed. Take it from me, the comparison is apt. I have studied his death mask from every angle.

Those with closed minds, non-believers, often marvel at my perspicacity in dealings with them and the delightful irony is, of course, that they are pig-headed, almost literally. Reason's presence, or absence, shapes the forehead. Mine is wide and curved; but enough about me.

You might be surprised to learn how many apparently respectable medical men are also attracted to this so-called pseudo-science. One such apparently respectable medic is Dr Neil Hunter, a forensic pathologist at the Police Mortuary in Edinburgh, and, fortunately, his area of acquisitiveness makes mine seem positively atrophied. He and I have corresponded over the years and, calling in a favour – twice I have passed on a much sought-after issue of *The Phrenological Journal and Magazine of Moral Science* (nos 184 and 244) – I requested a copy of Professor Anstruther's post mortem report. After I reminded him that crime is a public matter and that the report must have been produced at the trial, he could think of no good reason to withhold it from me. Should any qualms suddenly assail him, I mentioned, in passing, that I had another sought after *PJMMS* (no. 342) in my possession. I could almost hear him licking his lips down the phone. Regrettably, he had not been involved in that case, but would make it his business to find out who had been, and get a copy of the post mortem. Immediately he remembered that only days ago he had, by chance, seen the indictment relating to the case in the office. He could post it to me. Would that be of any use?

Indeed it would.

Chatty by nature and, possibly, expecting more crumbs from my table, he speculated that a post mortem would have been ordered in the case to ascertain the precise cause of death as, I now understand, being as old as Methuselah will no longer do. Nowadays, people do not die of 'old age.' How fortunate we all are! Later he phoned to say that he had heard that one of the Professor's *billets doux* from the Bad Blood Brigade had been found near the body and it was that, in this case, which had given Scotland's finest pause for thought, nudged them towards the scalpel. If I had *PJMMS* (no. 209), Hunter would, I do not doubt, have swopped it for the man's preserved heart had I requested the same. Gollum-like, he is beyond redemption.

Post Mortem report on Professor Sir Alexander David Anstruther, formerly residing at 45 Duddingston Lane, Edinburgh. The Post Mortem was executed by Dr Guy Beamish under the authority of Ailsa Watson, Procurator Fiscal of Edinburgh.

SUMMARY OF CLINICAL HISTORY:

The deceased was a 90-year-old caucasian male (DOB 28/4/1924) with no significant past medical history other than hypertension.

He was found at his home at about 8.30 a.m. on 7th June 2014 by a local authority contract employee, Mrs Irma Brown, who phoned 999 and the ambulance service attended her call. When found, the deceased was in his bed lying with his face upwards, head resting on a pillow. He was wearing striped pyjamas. Beside the bed, on the floor by his head, was another pillow. His bedding appeared otherwise normal and not disarranged. On forensic examination one surface of the pillow on the floor was noted to have minuscule traces of some slightly blood-stained saliva on it (submitted for forensic examination). The deceased was pronounced dead at 9.05 a.m. by attending paramedics and no resuscitation was attempted. He had been last seen alive at about 7 p.m. on 6th June 2014 by a neighbour, Miss Elaine Grey, who saw him at his window as she was passing his house.

DESCRIPTION OF GROSS LESIONS:
EXTERNAL EXAMINATION:

The body is that of a 90-year-old male. On measurement his height was 152.4 cm. He weighed 50.80 kg. His head hair was grey and sparse. He had brown eyes and his pupils were equal and 4 mm in diameter. Very minor arcus senilis was present around the irises. There is a slight pallor of the skin around the mouth and nose. His nose and nares were otherwise unremarkable on examination. The teeth in his lower jaw were mostly natural with occasional teeth missing and showed quite good hygiene. A partial denture was fitted in his upper jaw. His tongue and gums were unremarkable but there were signs of moderate bruising with associated lacerations in the inner aspect of his upper and lower lips. There were 2 lacerations on the inner aspects of both the upper and the lower lips, each approximately 3–4 mm in maximum dimension. His face and neck were clean-shaven and he had no scars or distinguishing marks. His chest musculature showed signs of wasting and on it were two blue and white adhesive electrode pads (35 mm in diameter), one situated below each clavicle. The distribution of his grey body and pubic hair was normal. He exhibited an 8 cm appendectomy scar in the left iliac fossa. His penis was uncircumcised and both testes were visible in the scrotum. The skin of the back and the anus was unremarkable. The upper limbs were symmetrical, with poorly developed musculature. Keratotic lesions were visible on both distal forearms and hands. His hands were otherwise unremarkable and showed close cut fingernails. His lower limbs were symmetrical and showed poorly developed musculature. He had a few small scars on both shins, no tattoos or other significant scarring or distinguishing marks. His shins were hairless below mid-shin level and his ankles exhibited a minor degree of oedema. His feet were unremarkable with good hygiene and closely trimmed toenails.

POST MORTEM CHANGES:

The deceased body has been refrigerated, rigor mortis is generalised and intense. Post Mortem lividity has a typical posterior distribution with contact pallor over the shoulder blades, buttocks and calves. There are no features of decomposition present.

INTERNAL EXAMINATION (BODY CAVITIES):

The right and left pleural cavity contains 10 ml of clear fluid with no adhesions. The pericardial sac is yellow, glistening without adhesions or fibrosis and contains 30 ml of a straw-coloured fluid. There is minimal fluid in the peritoneal cavity.

HEART: The heart is large with a normal shape and a weight of 450 grams. The pericardium is intact. The epicardial fat is diffusely firm. Upon opening the heart was grossly normal without evidence of myocardial infarction. The left ventricle measures 2.2 cm in thickness, the right ventricle measures 0.2 cm, the tricuspid ring measures 11 cm in circumference, the pulmonic right measures 8 cm, the mitral ring measures 10.2 cm, and the aortic ring measures 7 cm. The foramen ovale is closed. The circulation is left dominant. Examination of the great vessels of the heart reveals a degree of atherosclerosis consonant with the patient's age, with the area of greatest stenosis (60% luminal narrowing) at the bifurcation of the LAD.

AORTA: There is considerable atherosclerosis with measurable plaques along the full length of the ascending and descending aorta.

LUNGS: The right lung weighed 630 grams, the left weighed 710 grams. The lungs were both moderately congested with minor associated oedema. The lung parenchyma is pink with evidence of petechiae. The bronchi are grossly normal.

GASTROINTESTINAL SYSTEM: The oesophagus and stomach are normal in appearance without evidence of ulcers or varices. The stomach contains approximately 200 ml of thin, beige-coloured fluid but no identifiable food residue. The pancreas has a normal lobular cut surface with evidence of autolysis. The duodenum, ileum, jejunum and colon are all grossly normal without evidence of abnormal vasculature but exhibiting diverticuli. The appendix is absent. The liver weighs 2850g and the cut surface reveals a normal liver with no fibrosis present grossly. The gallbladder is in place with a probe patent bile duct through to the ampulla of Vater.

RETICULOENDOTHELIAL SYSTEM: The spleen is large weighing 340 grams, the cut surface reveals a normal-appearing white and red pulp. A number of abnormally large lymph nodes were noted.

GENITOURINARY SYSTEM: The right kidney weighs 200 grams, the left weighs 210 grams. The left kidney contains a 1.0 x 1.0 x 1.0 cm simple cyst containing a clear fluid. The cut surface reveals a normal-appearing cortex and medulla with intact calyces. The prostate and seminal vessels were cut revealing an enlarged prostate. Bladder mucosa appears congested. A small amount of blood-stained foul-smelling urine remained in the bladder.

ENDOCRINE SYSTEM: The adrenal glands are in the normal position and weigh 8.0 grams on the right and 11.6 grams on the left. The cut surface of the adrenal glands reveals a normal-appearing cortex and medulla. The thyroid gland weighs 12.4 grams and is grossly normal.

CLINICOPATHOLOGIC CORRELATION:

The patient was found face up on a pillow, apparently dead. Circumferential oral and nasal pallor were present. Bruising and lacerations to the inside of the upper and lower lips is in keeping with compression against the teeth. Traces of blood-stained saliva were found on one of the pillows. Taken together, these findings raise the possibility of smothering pressure to the face and lips. The mechanism of death proposed is asphyxia by smothering. Forensic scientific analysis of the pillow is suggested.

SUMMARY:

Cause of death 1 (A): Asphyxia by smothering.

Other relevant findings: Alzheimer's disease and urinary infection.

THIRD NARRATIVE *by*
ANTHONY SPARROW

A smothering? Somehow, I had not expected that although, on reflection, I should have. A pillow is a woman's weapon.

Having trudged my entire way through this semi-literate, jargon-filled work whilst lying, immobile, in my now tepid bath, I considered it would be to my advantage to speak to 'Darling Irma', 'Rough Andrea' and the fragrant Jean. I rose like Aphrodite from her shell, dripped, then shook myself like a dog before stepping out, gingerly, onto the bathmat. There are, you may be pleased to learn, no full-length mirrors in my own small, pink bathroom. Sleepless in bed, my cat, Fang Shui, by me, purring on the pillow, I cogitated until midnight, working out my strategy.

The next day, I had little difficulty in tracking down the first two through the Council, then the wages department of their employers. This I did by masquerading in the shabby agency office as an Inland Revenue inspector, suggesting that they were in arrears and had flitted from their last residences to avoid payment. Despite my lack of identification, the overweight, T-shirted young gentleman, masticated egg and cress sandwich in his gaping mouth, fell over himself in his eagerness to help me. A thin ruse, but quite sufficient, if combined with a voice that brooks no contradiction, to get around the much-vaunted Data Protection Act.

Once I learnt their whereabouts I visited each at their homes with a suitable 'keepsake', supposedly from Professor Anstruther, murmuring something about his 'final wishes'. For 'Rough Andrea' I chose the silver-backed hairbrushes, as she appeared to consider them her own before his demise, and for Irma I chose the Professor's complete set of gardening tools, all but brand new. Irma I found, in her fleshy way, magnificent. The Professor must have felt safe in her company, fit and shapely as a Russian javelin thrower. Should he fall, she could have scooped him up with one arm. Biceps on her like Popeye, tattoos to rival his, too. No mechanical aids would have been needed, just her comforting bulk, strong back, to heave him here and there. I see her, in my imagination, as a vast uniformed nurse, her tiny charge, puppet-like, perched on her knee.

I also took a closed cardboard box with other potential keepsakes in it, explaining that I was very interested in the circumstances of their former employer's death and now had complete discretion to distribute any other of his possessions as I saw fit. I muttered something about 'everything having fallen to me' and hoped they would assume some form of attenuated blood relationship. They seemed to take the hint, Irma choosing a porcelain shepherdess (of little value – 'Copenhagen' but made in Germany?) and Andrea opting, with a little pressure from myself, for a silver fob watch (no hallmarks). Andrea had mystery to her; a Mona Lisa-like enigma, albeit one with rough, red hands. A tall woman, shy, the sort who hold themselves slightly hunched to disguise their height. Gardening tools, shepherdess or nay, I don't think she liked me. Looking at me, the pupils in her pale eyes shut down to pinholes. I feel, if she could, she would have handled me with tongs. Pity, her occiput was so well-rounded, so attractive (a testament to her motherliness) that I would like to have photographed it.

Talking to them separately in their respective sitting rooms (oddly alike), I recorded our conversation, later that same day transcribing their contributions to my own satisfaction. Whatever they may have made of me, they both struck me as good, kind women and I should consider myself exceptionally fortunate if, as I crumble, I end up being cared for by such a pair. The picture they painted of Alexander Anstruther was of a proud little fellow, flesh failing, memory leaking like a sieve, increasingly reliant on Post-it notes and scraps of paper. Scared, too.

On reflection, Andrea would, I regret, probably draw the line at tending me. Some do. Nonetheless, I hope neither of them are called into the Agency office because of my ruse. If they are, they may not, I suppose, associate my visit with the curt inspector's inquiries. After all, why should they? I am almost inclined to phone the Agency in my persona as tax inspector and restore their reputations, only I cannot think of any way of doing so without incriminating myself. It will all blow over.

Having spoken to them, I concluded that a visit to Prof. Eileen Coates might also prove instructive, and I tracked down her address via the Medical Register.

Unfortunately, she died in December 2014. Her daughter, Bridget, square-footed, shod in brown brogues and now ensconced in solitary New Town splendour, seemed overjoyed, if surprised, to receive her 'legacy'; the Prof's tweed Inverness cape. Of optimistic disposition, she seemed sure it would fit. I had made a good choice, as its heathery hue, I noted, matched her complexion to a T. In passing it to her on its coat-hanger, I tried to chat to her about the donor and, as I suspect she is lonely, she humoured me for a couple of minutes until the piano tuner for her baby grand arrived at the appointed time. Before his breakdown, she told me in hushed tones in her kitchen, nodding excitedly as if to emphasise the fact, he had been the Manager of the Balmoral Hotel. Imagine that? Hundreds of staff at his beck and call! A pale middle-aged man passed the doorway on his way to the Music Room, and my intuition tells me she has matrimonial designs on the fellow. Why not? She did her duty, may be a significant heiress too. And harmony, of some sort, might be her reward. With the Steinway incapacitated, Jammy Dodgers appear to be the food of love. Once I got home, I jotted down what I could remember, in note form, of our brief, interrupted conversation.

The next day, I opened the post at breakfast and found Dr Hunter had been as good as his word. A blue envelope contained the indictment, couched in its semi-impenetrable officialese, for my delectation. Naturally, I append it below for yours, and apologise for the coffee-cup stain. The view that I take is that, following the same path, step by step, we should reach our destination together. So far, my dainty size 8s tread, page-like, in the Plod's size 15s.

Whilst bolting the remains of my first bagel and honey (I was going to be late for a meeting at Anstruther's house with some carriers), sticky-fingered, I consulted Dr Google requesting any newspaper reports on the case, and I append the ones he found for me below. I did not do this originally as (a) I do not trust him; (b) having the man's own story, I did not want to be influenced by anyone else's. Not that I am easily swayed. No. By inclination, I dislike moving with the herd, visualise them as thousands of shaggy gnus, giddy, teetering, jostling to jump off the cliff, stilt-legs pedalling desperately as they fall into the open jaws of the crocodiles waiting in the river below. This gnu walks alone. What I am at pains to explain, I suppose, is how conscious I was that, unlike anyone else, I had heard the man's unmediated voice. A privilege of sorts, albeit an odd one, and one which required its reception with a completely open mind.

As I was continuing my newspaper research on the computer, a call from a fellow bibliophile distracted me, made me drop my knife on the floor. Immediately, Fang Shui jumped off my lap and started licking the blade with his rough tongue.

'Anthony?'

'Yes.' I knew that German intonation, was immediately put on guard. An image of the man's 'retail outlet' in Nantwich, more properly his den, elbowed its way into my mind. So dark, so dusty. Ideal for passing off fakes as genuine to credulous or cataract-ridden amateurs. And the man's head is always hidden in a deerstalker. Need I say more?

'I was wondering about something, my dear,' he wheezed, 'a little gift for you? Would you like to see Spurzheim's *The Physiognomical System of Drs Gall and Spurzheim*? I know you're looking, and can you believe my luck, I've come across two copies, I'm keeping one, and you came to mind . . .'

'How kind, but I'm in the process of acquiring one myself,' I lied without qualm, manoeuvring Fang Shui off his treat lightly with a stockinged foot.

'But . . . mint condition . . .'

'Must go, Tomas, bye.'

'It'd be quite reasonable, Anthony . . .'

I should cocoa.

'By good fortune, I'm in Edinburgh for the day, no distance away . . .' he wheedled.

To save myself from myself, I said, 'Oh, what a pity. Unfortunately, I'm not,' and put the phone down.

Of course it was no gift, I knew that. One might as well call a Grouse and Claret flicked over a lochan trout's lips a gift. It is a lure, intended to catch the fish, hook the fish. And Tomas Leipi knew his prey, had cast well. I itched to see the book, was beginning to think I should ring back when I noticed black smoke issuing from my defective grill, my supplementary bagel on fire. Cursing, I jumped up, grabbed last night's frying pan and began beating the flames with it.

That was when I rested my coffee cup on the indictment.

Thinking about things now, I realise should have deferred speaking to those women until I had read the newspaper reports that I attach below. But there it is, I did not. Perhaps if I had, I would have incurred my informants' suspicion, appearing insufficiently ignorant and insufficiently discreet and, somehow, inadvertently revealed my clandestine purpose. More likely, I would not have felt the need to speak to them at all. My excuse is that I am an amateur, a talented one, but nonetheless an amateur.

I attach the jottings and statements for your interest below.

INDICTMENT
(provided by Dr Neil Hunter)
Section 76 WW12874030
Dated 20 August 2014

Jean Mary Whitadder, born on 16 January 1984, whose domicile of citation has been specified as 15A Riley Drive, Niddrie, you are indicted at the instance of Her Majesty's Advocate, and the charge against you is that sometime between 6 June 2014 and 7 June 2014 at number 45 Duddingston Lane, Edinburgh, you Jean Mary Whitadder did assault Alexander David Anstruther, residing there, did place a pillow over his face and forcibly hold it there, thereby restricting his breathing and you did kill him.

NMIL/KL/LM
PF ref: WW 12874030
2014
High Court
Edinburgh
Criminal Procedure (Scotland) Act 1995
Section 76

STATEMENT

of

Andrea Lewis

(20th May 2017)

I am employed by the Norris Care Agency and we do work for the Council. I go to about fifteen different clients, travelling between them though the agency allows me no time, or money, for travel and if I get caught in traffic or something no one gets their full allowance of time. No petrol money for me either. Some of the clients deliberately hold you back, eat very slowly or ask for last-minute tasks, desperate for the company. Mainly I do old people although I've one mentally challenged and a Down's. I've got no contract but as my Shelley's got kids, I don't mind. I can take time off if the kids are ill or there's a custody hearing against Mandy's ex-partner. The wee one's got haemophilia so he's quite often off nursery. It upsets me so much I don't talk about it unless I have to. My brother died of a bleed, thanks to it.

I started working for Sir Alexander in early 2011. Old

Mrs Davidson moved into a home and I was put on his run. He lives in Duddingston Village and that suited me OK as I can often park in the churchyard or the pub car park. I, usually, did him either in the morning or in the evenings. He got 20 minutes each time. He was 90, wasn't in bad nick for such an age. At first, he seemed a doddle, needed things done just so, pernickety, but otherwise fine. Like he wouldn't eat the sandwiches I'd make for him unless all the crusts were taken off, even with sliced bread. I'd water his plants, maybe do a bit of washing up and so on. That big place was always icy cold, he wore coats sometimes, even inside. Gloves a few times. After a bit, he was getting a bit odd, I thought. Sometimes he'd ask me to do things I'm not supposed to do. After Lucky died he was lonely, I reckon. I don't know exactly when he changed, but it'd be about the time he took on that Jean Whitadder as a cleaner. He seemed a bit soft on her, like some old men get. Too soft, if you ask me. Personally, I had a flasher myself once. I only met Whitadder the one time, of course, because we rarely coincided but, God almighty, I heard all about her, too much about her. He could rabbit on about her for Scotland. She never left the crusts on, didn't drown the plants, blah, blah, but she wasn't rushing from the last client and scurrying to the next one, always late, always chasing her tail. I don't know who she worked for, I don't think it was an agency. All I know is she did things 'properly', didn't need to be told all the time. Never filled in the record either, and that's not right. Soft on her, he was. The only time we met, she was doing something to his pills. I told her off, told her they'd nothing to do with her, but she just stared at me with a death stare and carried on, putting pills into the wrong bottle. I reported her to the office, that's how I know she wasn't an agency worker. We're told never to touch the clients' medication unless they specially ask us. It could be dangerous. What was she doing?

Not long after she came, he got a bit ratty and started accusing, not directly, but accusing me of things. Hiding stuff. He even sort of hinted that I was pilfering, but odd things, things I'd never even want, old teapots, pens. We use teabags in cups, what would I want with an old blackened teapot? Now I know she took the tat he was complaining about. After she came, someone broke his window with a brick. I don't usually see Irma but I phoned her up one day as he seemed so difficult, she said she'd near enough had enough, was going to have it out with the office. But we can't pick and choose. Of course, Jean could do no wrong. I don't like to say this but from the moment she came, he seemed to change, became neurotic about everything. I wondered if she was playing tricks on him, upsetting him in some way, trying to unsettle him as he took to muttering to himself constantly. He was unhappy, the poor old dear, and always anxious, afraid almost. Said someone was after him. I thought it was the dementia coming, 'cause I've seen that plenty before. The whole place was full of old papers, filling up with them, piles everywhere, he'd got funny about papers. You could hardly move. I tried to get him re-assessed, he was failing and I thought if the Council would give him one more helper, maybe he'd get rid of her. See, he was pretty weak, his balance was all but gone and I didn't think he was safe on his own anymore. After it happened the police asked me all sorts of questions. As I said, he'd been going downhill – doolally? – for a while, I've seen the signs often enough. They even asked me if I had done it, because I put him to bed. He told me Jean was coming for a visit and I got the impression he was going to give her a piece of his mind, maybe even give her cards to her. She'd been skiving on and off, pulling a sickie here and there. My DNA was on the pillow too. Well, it would be, wouldn't it! They also asked about Jean, Irma too, and in the end, when they came back, asked me direct who I thought had done it. I told the truth. Jean, I said. I wouldn't be surprised because in the last few days he seemed to turn on her, see through her, listen more to me. He was spitting. I think she was at it. I think she was trying to get her claws into him, a frail old man with money. He may have torn a strip off her. Like I said, I once caught her putting his pills in the wrong container. She maintained he'd told her to, but he knew nothing about it. The wrong pills can kill you. I asked him, of course. I went to his funeral, so did Irma, but she didn't. Says it all, no family, a couple of friends on sticks, the lawyer, me and Irma. But not her, of course. Money, she was after his money and I saw that on day one. Whatever she may say, and I don't believe a word of it. Throw away the key, I say.

STATEMENT
of
Irma Brown
(20th May 2017)

I've worked for the Professor for about two years. I'm employed by Norris's and we work for the Council, you know, the new scheme to keep old folks in their homes? I was there 20 minutes, sometimes in the morning, sometimes in the evening, whatever the office told me. You get no warning either, they shuffle you about like playing cards. They need to get their act together.

I liked him but he wasn't always that easy. I suppose he was used to giving orders, not taking them. Like, he was feeding Lucky rotten smelly meat, but he wouldn't listen to me, carried on, and did for the poor old mutt. I had to throw out about fourteen tins from his cupboard and the smell would turn your stomach. I worried what she was eating, chocolate eclairs, fruitcake and so on. After I'd been there a fair bit, he became difficult, suspicious, not like his old self. I'd date it to when Jean arrived, he seemed OK before her ladyship came. She was to be a sort of 'Daily Help Secretary', he said. Not that you'd know it with all those papers everywhere cluttering up the place. I've been caring for a long time and I've met her type before, nice as ninepence at first, a bit too nice, if you know what I mean, particularly to old men. See, if they've a pretty face, the men don't bother if they've not done the dusting or whatever, they can still do no wrong. Several times he told me off, but they were jobs she ought to have done. I hardly ever met her but I got sick of the sound of her name. It was all Jean this, Jean that. I don't know what she did exactly, but cleaning didn't seem to be any part of it. He had her going through papers and things.

He accused me, right out, of taking his cufflinks! My partner never wears those kinds of shirts, I don't know what gave him the idea. That happened to me once before, the old lady had to go into a home soon after. Nothing to do with me, mind. He was getting a bit funny, too, by the end. Mumbling, muttering and so on. He seemed to be terrified of something. I thought maybe he'd got the flu those last few days, something serious, he was that weak, feverish maybe. He'd papers everywhere, but he wouldn't let me touch them. They were for the court thing, I think. Only her ladyship was good enough for that. The police came and saw me after he died, asked me all about him and Jean. At first, I thought they thought I'd done it! I told them straight away that I reckoned that Jean was up to something – too cosy, too familiar by half, judging by what he said. Pinching things, anyway, and maybe he caught her at it? In the act. What I do know is she didn't need to use the key-safe to get in, 'cause I asked her the combination one time after it had been changed. No idea, she'd her own key, you see. How did she get that, I wonder? She could help herself to anything, come in while he was asleep or whatever. There were no checks on her by any agency, no training, no flies either, as she was sharp as a knife. My DNA was on the pillow, but so was hers, and Andrea's for that matter. Why was hers? I had to give an 'elimination' sample. Only me and Andrea were supposed to put him to bed. I found him the next morning. I thought he was asleep, sometimes he was that slow to wake, but when I came back with his tray and tapped his shoulder I realised my mistake alright. I phoned 999, then the agency, to see what I was supposed to do. I phoned my partner, Dougie, too, he told me to calm down, relax, etc., and that help would come soon. He's a fitness coach. I was with Dr Anstruther – well, the body, really, until the ambulance men came. Blue light, too, as if it could make a bit of difference. Sometimes I think these people must just be bored or rushing for their tea. I'll never forget what happened, I was off for a week with my nerves. I may have PTSD, I've tablets to help me forget. He's the only dead body I've ever seen.

NOTES OF CONVERSATION
WITH BRIDGET COATES

Mummy was heartbroken, killed her . . . old chums, colleagues for years . . . awful thing to happen to anybody, Mummy might have married him, second time round, you know, he was very gallant, attentive . . . never liked the girl . . . a dreadful little minx . . . what was she doing there . . . no respect for Mummy, self or Professor Anstruther . . . blue blood, my foot [?] . . . put phone down on me, once, twice . . . he was so frail, so vulnerable . . . no more a cleaner than I am . . . glad Mummy not alive to see mess the world in . . . people like her inveigle way into lives . . . sign of the times.

Printout from *The Times* newspaper of 15 June 2014

CARE WORKER ACCUSED OF MURDERING JUDICIAL INQUIRY WITNESS

A Care Assistant accused of suffocating the elderly man whom she was employed to care for stayed all but silent in Court this morning as she denied his murder. Jean Mary Whitadder, allegedly suffocated the elderly physician, Professor Sir Alexander Anstruther, with a pillow at his multi-million-pound home in Duddingston Village, Edinburgh.

The 90-year-old man, a former Professor of Haematology Medicine at the University of Edinburgh, was found dead in his own bed by another of his carers, Ms Irma Brown. On the morning that he was found, he was due to continue giving evidence to the Goodhart Inquiry, a Judicial Inquiry set up by the Scottish Government to look into the contamination of the public blood supply by HIV/AIDS. It is believed that his part in the 'Tainted Blood' scandal was pivotal and his evidence was eagerly awaited by many, including the 'Bad Blood Brigade', a particularly vociferous group of victims. Whitadder, from the nearby Riley estate in Niddrie, appeared at Edinburgh Sheriff Court this morning and entered no plea or declaration to the charge of murder. With her arms crossed throughout, Whitadder confirmed her name in a low voice but remained silent when the charge was put to her and a solicitor spoke on her behalf. Peter Benjamin, the presiding Sheriff, remanded Whitadder in custody until her trial.

The Times, 20 August 2014

CARER ACCUSED OF MURDERING HER EMPLOYER

A woman suffocated her frail elderly employer in his own home, the High Court in Edinburgh was told yesterday.

The jury was also shown footage of the accused walking away from the man's home at 8.55 p.m., about eleven hours before the 90-year-old's body was found face up on his pillow, the covers around his neck and wearing his pyjamas.

The evidence was given to the High Court of Justiciary in Edinburgh yesterday in the trial of Jean Whitadder, 30, who has been charged with murdering the unmarried former Professor of Haematology Medicine at his Georgian home in Duddingston Village sometime between the 6th and 7th of June, 2014.

Prosecuting Counsel, Josephine Quick QC, had previously told the court that Ms Whitadder, a former barmaid, had applied for a job as Professor Anstruther's carer in response to an advert he had placed in the *Scotsman* newspaper.

Whitadder, of 15a Riley Drive, Niddrie, Edinburgh, has pleaded not guilty to the charge of murder.

A paramedic, Robert White, testified that he was called to the former manse at about 9 a.m. and found Professor Anstruther's body lying in his bed.

'When we found him, he had no apparent marks on him,' he said. 'On the floor, immediately to the side of his bed, was a pillow. He had another pillow under his head.' He added that there appeared to be some semi-transparent excreted matter on the pillow that was found on the floor. 'There was an old-fashioned chamber pot directly under the bed,' he added.

Dr Guy Beamish, the police pathologist, testified that death was caused by asphyxia or lack of oxygen due to suffocation, quite possibly with the use of the deceased's own pillow. He described bruising and abrasions found on the inner surface of the Professor's lips as being consistent with suffocation.

From his examination at post mortem he could also tell that Professor Anstruther was suffering from the relatively early stages of Alzheimer's disease and that he may also have had a urinary tract infection at the time of his death and been in a confused state.

The jury was also shown a montage of CCTV footage gathered from the Duddingston Village location at the time.

P.C. Barry Marsden pointed out Ms Whitadder

arriving at the former manse at about 8 p.m. the night before the Professor was found. Earlier, the camera recorded her parking her Ford Focus nearby, opposite the Sheep's Heid public house. The next clip was captured as she returned to her car. Her walk was slow and she appeared to have a leather-bound book in her hand. The book, found later when Ms Whitadder's home was searched, was 'A Family History of the Anstruthers of Strathdonald'. Other possessions, including a silver teapot, gold cufflinks, a bracelet in the shape of linked owls and silver candlesticks, belonging to Professor Anstruther, were also found in the premises in Niddrie.

'You can see Ms Whitadder arriving, and leaving, in her work overalls,' he said. P.C. Marsden pointed out that Ms Whitadder had put a beanie hat on by the time she was seen returning to her vehicle in the rain. That footage was timed at 8 55 p.m.

'She seems to be covering her face or wiping her face with a tissue,' P.C. Marsden observed.

A witness, Ms Andrea Lewis, another of Professor Anstruther's carers, told the Court that she had become worried about the relationship developing between the elderly man and his new carer. 'I advised him to get references from her,' she said, 'but, once he saw her, he never did anything about it.' She described how things seemed to go missing after Ms Whitadder arrived, including antique silver.

'I think,' she said, 'she was taking advantage of him.

At first, he talked about her all the time, as if he could not believe his good luck. He even had her doing paperwork for him, signing things and so on because it was difficult for him with his shaky hand and everything. I think she was cosying up to him, worming her way in, he was lonely and she knew it. Once I saw flowers and he said she'd given them to him. He was giggly, seemed to think it was marvellous. You see, he'd lost the plot . . . well, he was losing it.'

Another carer, Ms Irma Brown, recalled that, shortly before he died, the professor's attitude to Ms Whitadder changed, and he seemed afraid of her.

'There was nothing I could put my finger on,' she said, 'but he looked fearful just at the mention of her name. He also seemed cross with her, although I'm not sure why exactly. Mind you, he wasn't himself by the end.'

Evidence was also given by Ronald Menzies WS, a lawyer with the George Street firm of Kennedy and Irons. He explained that he was new to the job, Professor Anstruther's long-term family lawyer having died suddenly. In answer to a question by the Prosecuting Counsel, he replied that on 1st June 2014 he had opened a communication from the deceased containing a new will, signed by the deceased where required and witnessed in accordance with all the necessary formalities. 'It was identical to the earlier one, except Ms Whitadder was now also to benefit from the Estate,' he said. 'Previously, in terms of the old will, this very substantial Estate was to be divided, a third each, between the Haemophilia Society,

Haemophilia Scotland, the MRC and the Langford Trust. In terms of the new will I was to pay three-eighth shares between them all, with the remainder, five-eighths, to go to the new beneficiary, Jean Whitadder. The sooner the Professor died, the sooner the beneficiaries, including Miss Whitadder, received her money.'

The trial continues.

FOURTH NARRATIVE *of*
ANTHONY SPARROW

My mind full of the murderous Whitadder hussy, I clattered across the city in my battered blue Polo to meet the carriers at Anstruther's house in Duddingston. Needless to say, throughout my entire journey, I saw nothing of Stockbridge, George Street, the cobbles of St Mary's Street, the Pleasance or anywhere else. One minute I was outside my flat in Dean Street, the next I was halfway across Holyrood Park. The knowledge of that complete blank both scares and mystifies me. Fully conscious and alert, I am a bad driver, have nearly been put off the road twice, and confess, to my shame, to killing a giant Schnauzer. However, few would dispute (I'd wager) that attending to one's toilet on a blind summit is unwise. Red lights, give-ways, roundabouts, pedestrian crossings? How I do not have more blood on my bonnet, I will never know. I saw and heard nothing, because that woman, and nothing but that woman, filled my mind. I argued with her, or myself, questioned her aggressively, wondered, shivered at her brutality, cold bloodedness, pictured the old man's frailty and his end. I did not even feel my thumb and first finger, both burnt when I flung the blackened, smoking bagel into the kitchen sink.

Finally, I came to, you might say, with my seatbelt alarm

penetrating my eardrums, my eyes registering the sight of a family of ducks, a mother and five infants, waddling across the road in front of me. I jammed my foot down. The brakes squealed like a banshee but, mercifully, the sextet reached the other side in safety, bodies and souls together.

Automatic pilot or not, I hit my destination at the appointed hour. Were the eager tradesmen awaiting me there? Were they buggery. The next five minutes were spent examining my damaged digits, one already blistered, and muttering to myself about Messrs Reed and Stenton. From my parking spot overlooking the loch, I further whiled away my time watching the waterside life: a few desultory walkers and one youth staring fixedly at the summit of Arthur's Seat as if expecting an imminent eruption. To my left, a gaggle of Chinese geese were terrorising a little girl, hissing, stretching their necks like snakes in her direction, making her scream so piercingly that the noise penetrated my cocoon. As the mother, a sylph in a lilac scarf, suddenly realised what was happening, she began to clap her hands, advancing on the birds as a human shield. One thick-necked gander, up for the fray, advanced towards her, wings outstretched. Unexpectedly, I heard myself starting to hiss in chorus with him.

As at that exact moment, the Carrier's rusty Pan Techni-con crunched its way over the gravel, unfortunately I never saw the final act in that little drama. My money, however, would be on the gander. Punctuality being well above God-liness as far as I am concerned, I had already decided that, however cheap their quote was, Reed and Stenton would not get the job. After a protracted ding-dong with their mulish gaffer in the inner hall of the manse, I could feel my systems closing down in the gelid air. His too, judging by the colour of his nose, not to mention the drip on its end.

'It was the accident at Barnton made us late . . .' he repeated for the third time.

'I don't care.'

'But it was the accident, Mr Sparrow.'

'Accident. Shmaccident.'

'Eh?'

'Time waits for no man.'

'Right. Like I said, we've a special deal on – cheaper than Dunbar, Morton's, any of those . . .'

'Oh, very well, I will think about your d . . . d . . . deal,' I spat, worn out, determined to end the exchange, expel the fellow and get on with my cataloguing task.

'If accepted before noon, there'll be a discount.'

Never enough, I thought, but did not say.

To ensure his immediate departure, I led him across the gravel and the cobbled street, right to the door of his heated cab, deposited him there and then sped back indoors to the cold.

In the library I was reunited with my flask of hot coffee, and, cradling my plastic beaker to my breast, managed to stave off the incipient hypothermia that had made my teeth chatter and relieved me of all feeling in my toes. With the grains still bitter on my tongue, I set to work, determined to, finally, clear my mind of Jean Whitadder and warm myself up. Perhaps the mystery had indeed been solved; no more of my time or precious energy needed to be spent on it. Brisk movement, I had decided, might force the blood around my circulatory system, heat me from the inside out and redden the blanched tips of my fingers. So I patrolled the shelves, hopping from foot to foot, flapping my arms against my sides like an irate penguin defending its territory. Glimpsing myself in the mirror, I laughed out loud: tramp's coat covering my bowed back, woolly, fingerless gloves and a vapour trail issuing from a sinister head, one encased in a black cashmere snood. Looking rather more like a beetle than usual, in fact.

Zigzagging my way towards the unlit fireplace, I noticed, crushed into a crevice between the last volume of Murray's 1832 edition of Byron's Works and the wooden upright, a copy of Antoine St Exupery's *Little Prince*. A modern version printed in 2001 by Egmont and, really, of very little interest to me in monetary terms. All but worthless. On the other hand, Anstruther had mentioned it in his journal, and there was something inserted in it, distorting the little paperback and weakening its spine. A homemade bookmark? Worthless or not, books should not be maltreated. It was the work of a second to remove the foreign object. It turned out to be a thick, unopened envelope addressed to Miss Jean Whitadder and marked 'To be delivered by hand' in writing that I recognised immediately.

As you must have gathered, I am not the sort of man to have any compunction about opening other people's letters, particularly if a correspondent is dead. Quite the reverse; when I 'clear' I glory (I choose my words with care) in my liberty to bring everything out into the open, into the light. At least to satisfy my professional curiosity or, others might say, nosiness. The letter that I discovered is reproduced below as Document A. It contained twenty crisp ten-pound notes, and I found it oddly moving to see, once more, the Professor's trembly, blot-spattered handwriting. It was as if he was trying to communicate with me again, egg me on. Exhort me from the grave not to give up.

Having read his letter, it dawned on me that I had the perfect excuse to meet Miss Whitadder. And why not? My curiosity had been piqued by her for long enough, my time was my own and I had my reasons, idiosyncratic or not. Others had seen her, listened to her and reached their own conclusions; why should I not do the same? Also, such a meeting should, I reckoned, finally release the strange hold she still had on me. It would be a form of exorcism, bring 'closure', and if the plods were vindicated, so be it. Occasionally, they must be right.

I contacted the woman through the prison authorities, but she declined my initial, rather impersonal overture. However, I hooked her on my second attempt by using a postcard providing her with an incomplete description of the letter and suggesting that the rest of its contents might be of particular pecuniary interest to her, if I could only see her to hand it over. This time, she graciously acceded to my request.

We met in a large, ill-favoured communal meeting room in Saughton prison. The heat and stink of sweat mixed with cheap perfume in it all but made me gag. By then I had undergone the indignity of a number of 'body-searches' and was a tad flustered, uneasy, on the edge of hyperventilating. I do not like being touched. Sensing my weakness, the woman appraised me, her eyes locking onto me un apologetically, almost impertinently. She was, undoubtedly, strikingly pretty – although in an oddly refined way, no blousy barmaid, she – but I am, as I have already admitted, largely immune to female charms in all their diverse forms. Like a cat, she circled me. If forced to describe her, I would say she was a mixture of Eva Peron and some colleen dreamt up by the Irish Tourist Board. When her eyes had had their fill, she beckoned me towards a glass-topped table that had an orange plastic chair on either side of it.

Breathlessness apart, I suspect that my manner instantly annoyed her, as I cannot pretend that I did not view her almost as a specimen or a type. Perhaps she sensed this and it antagonised her. Who could blame her? In my defence, I had never, to my knowledge, cast my eye upon a murderess before in real life, and I was driven to observe such a physiognomy at first hand, for myself. From a phrenological perspective, I noticed that she showed none of the low-browed, heavy-jawed looks, suggestive of animal propensities, that one might expect of a killer, although, I must admit, again, to being a relative amateur in these matters. And perhaps it comes out differently in womenfolk? What George Combe or Bernard Hollander would have made of that head, I cannot say. Contrary to my prejudices, it was her keen intelligence that struck me most of all.

I had taken it as read that she would wish to converse with me, being sufficiently bored by her impoverished, malodorous environment, and possibly her companions, to feel the need to contact somebody new and of the outside world. Not a bit of it. Her large, cornflower-blue eyes exhibited no warmth or friendliness towards me, and when I confessed that I was interested in her case, was looking into it, she became even more monosyllabic than on first acquaintance. She took the copy of the letter that I proffered in her long-fingered hand without comment. Having read it, she inquired how it came to be in my possession; so I explained that, in accordance with Professor Anstruther's executor's instructions I was clearing his house, sorting through all his chattels. Those blue eyes became colder still, icily fixed on me. The two hundred pounds, I assured her, finding myself gabbling, awaited her instructions. It struck me then that in the film she might make of her own life with her as, say, a Cleopatra figure, I would appear (if I was lucky) as fifth Egyptian slave or Old Man with Pot Belly. Or, more likely, a fly. As an offering, I bought her a Snicker bar from the dispensing machine. Whilst I was mid-reverie, visualizing her kohl-eyed in a coal black wig, she rose from her chair as an empress might, dismissing me wordlessly. On cue, half the women in the room followed in her wake like track-suited, pony-tailed handmaidens. I left Saughton dejected and rueing the money I had wasted on diesel.

A good many months later a brown-paper parcel arrived (I have no idea how she discovered my address) and inside it was the notebook which will now feature in this narrative. Enclosed with it ~~with it~~ was a short note to me, written, to be frank, in an ugly, uneven script, but one with which I was to become familiar.

Saughton, 12th July 2017

Dear Mr Sparrow

Thank you for coming to visit me and for the chocolate you bought me from the machine. I enclose my notebook for you to look at. It is for your eyes ONLY. You have in your possession something that I want and which was given to me by the Professor. It is of little value to others including yourself. I should be grateful if you would let me have it. I think after you have read the enclosed notebook you will understand why I wish to have it returned to me.

cheers
Jean Whitadder

I have included below (Document B) typed extracts from Miss Whitadder's notebook, in so far as germane and covering the period with which we are concerned. On some of the pages were illustrations, done by her in inks, largely of street scenes, anchors and cats. Accomplished, they suggested that she had quite a rare talent for someone who, to the best of my knowledge, is untutored. There was also ephemera, a few pressed flowers, railway tickets and cinema tickets but, for obvious reasons, I have not attempted to have them copied. The document was hand-written and, in places, difficult to decipher, but I have typed it out and am satisfied that it is, to the best of my knowledge, accurate. All I have altered, where appropriate, is the spelling.

Document C (a psychiatric report prepared by Dr Andrew Harold dated 23rd August 2014) came into my possession through the good offices of the insatiable Dr Neil Hunter. Hearing from a mutual acquaintance that I had obtained a very rare monograph by George Combe he sent me it unasked with a note simply saying: 'One good deed deserves another?'

Gritting my teeth, I sent him the monograph. And, in a separate envelope, my bill.

DOCUMENT A

Primrose Bank
Duddingston
Edinburgh
29th April 2014

Dear Jean,

You have now been in my employ for over two months. Accordingly, your probationary period is over and I would like your employment with me to continue. As a token of

my satisfaction to date – a member of my own family (if
I had one!) could not be more attentive – I am enclosing
herewith the sum of £200 in cash.

Yours sincerely,
Alexander Anstruther.

DOCUMENT B

Extract from the
'Writing Notebook'
of
JEAN WHITADDER

2014

20th January

OMG, I've lost my job at The Beggars' Inn. Can you bloody
believe it! They've warned me before but I never thought
fat Al would actually do something. All I did was slip Lena
a couple of freebies, nothing expensive, Teachers maybe.
Or was it the Macallan? Cornford caught me last time,
must have been at least three months ago, and warned me
then, but he smiled, too, like he'd now got a hold over
me. Never thought he'd fire me, the nubbin. His bloodshot
eyes used to follow me wherever I went like a pair of puppy
dogs. Bubba won't stand in for me, on principle, he said,
but he will. Needs the money, you see. I was allowed to
collect my coat and bag (thank you kindly) and told that
I was not welcome back anytime soon. As if I'd drink

there anyway. The mark-up's diabolical and there's no bloody music allowed except piped Radio 2 crap. Half the customers are dead, or as good as, and the food's all from Iceland anyway. I should have reported Al Cornford to someone that time he trapped me against the kegs. It was like being crushed between two beer barrels. Having speedily necked as many tequilas as possible as I'll not get my wages, I may, possibly, have knocked the tap of the IPA on as I left. Oopsie! Phoned Lena and she chummed me home, half-cut, and she whistled at a passing scout. He smiled, flushed like a wee beetroot.

But how will me and Garry survive?

Ever since sixth form, I seem to have lost my way. Lena and her weed have been my downfall. That stuff she gave me burned my mind, made me too high for my Highers. Could I get a job with her with the Council? But a child-minder? *Moi*? Garry's more than enough for me. Cornford won't give me a reference although, I suppose, I could write myself one like the one I did for him? Or better. I am 'reliable and hard-working' and 'tidy and efficient'. Would 'a treasure' be going too far? Someone might phone him up, mind. I am slipping backwards all the time, going nowhere. I want to be SOMEBODY.

23rd January
Applied for a stop-gap job in a shoe shop but I'm glad I didn't get it. The smell. And I'm not sure I could handle (ha ha) too many old folk's bunions. Went to Portobello beach and walked along it, just looking at the great, gray

sea. I've always liked the sea, ever since me and Mum lived by it in Dunbar. In those old, high houses, right on the harbour, the sound of the kittiwakes always in your ears. Bird poo and litter covering the cobbles and the rocks. There'll be white gulls under, the shite cliffs of Dunbar.

Was nearly run over walking home. Some numpty further up the street's dog had got off its lead and the wee French bulldog was jinking in and out the traffic, dodging here and there like it was a game.

'Lola, Lola . . . you come right back here!' the woman bawled.

As it scampered past me I stepped on the road to grab it, just as a car mounted the pavement trying not to hit it. Lola's only got eight lives left, I saw her dash off into the park. She was lovely, big ears and a black and white coat. I'd like one of them. Garry would too.

30th January
Got a job in a Call Centre!

6th February
Well! What a day! Flying solo at last, I phoned this number to sell our kitchen units and I stuck, clam-like, to the dia-logue sheet. To the very word. Then, as I was talking about how we'd be in the man's area etc., the old fellow wheezed 'I'd like YOU in my area, girlie!' (or something). Alarm bells ringing, I ignored him and carried on saying we'd need to take measurements etc., and he said 'you'll have no cause to complain of my measurements!' I laughed out

loud and that just made him worse. I put the phone down. Then I got called in to the office and told off.

Four hours later, a woman said to me 'No, no sodding units and I'm on the TPS, so you can FUCK OFF', no sooner than I'd begun to speak. And without thinking, I said 'You an' all,' as I signed off. The man beside me, Robbie, says that for our first week on, all our calls are not only recorded but actually listened to by the supervisor. He says I'll be out for that. I am NOT being fired again, so I logged out and left. Seems like the story of my life, since the library 'let me go' due to the cuts, despite Mum's pleas. Somehow, they managed to keep Jakub, the stoned Pole, despite his pidgin Disses and Dats. Tonight, to cheer myself up, I'm going to that Council creative writing course again.

Malcolm was teaching, spaghetti legs in spray-on white jeans this time. He asked how many of us were keeping notebooks, and I put up my hand, and if we'd been listening to other people's conversations like he'd suggested. I put my hand up again. Our exercise was to write up the best one we'd heard.

I was on the top of the double-decker, behind this old couple in the front seat, and we were waiting at the bus stop as more passengers were getting in.

Him: (points to passing pedestrian) 'What's she doing out?'

Her: 'Who?'

Him: 'Her, that Eleanor . . . from the coffee place. She'd an amputation five minutes ago. Fudge?'

Her: 'Don't bare your teeth at her, Ron. You'll give her a fright.'

Him: 'It's an improvement, eh? smoother, nice colour . . .'

Her: 'Her new leg?'

Him: 'The fudge, the fudge.'

I read it out and Malcolm liked it, hovered over me. Later, he whispered, 'Like to go over your last exercise with me, one to one?'

As if. 'Sorry, got to charge my phone. Ta.' Blink, and he'll be a pensioner, crumbling to dust.

There are only women on this course and he struts about like a cockerel amongst the fowls, preening himself. Me and Garry shared a fish supper tonight. One day, Malcolm will beg me to sign one of my books for him.

17th February

Mum sent me a photo of an ad she saw in the *Scotsman*.

'Wanted: Assistant who is prepared to tackle a variety of different tasks including shopping, cleaning, cataloguing, precising, filing etc., for an elderly gentleman. Edinburgh area. Clean driving licence required. Pay and hours negotiable. Tel: 0131 888 444.'

What have I to lose? I am going nowhere anyway. I phoned up immediately and a crackly, snobby voice answered. I'm to go for an interview tomorrow and to bring my references. I'll have to rewrite them tonight. One speeding hardly counts, does it?

20th February

Today I had the interview. What a fab place! It's just an old white house but it looks right over Duddingston Loch. Frogs could jump in the windows. It's chokker with books, pictures and black mahogany antiques. Old-fashioned, waxy smelling. And there are papers everywhere, but when I tried to move a pile of them off the settee, just to sit down, the old man was having none of it. Talking about 'his system'. He showed me onto a bamboo chair. He must be very rich. If he offers it me, I'll take the job. He says there's a lot of filing, cataloguing and so on but I can do that. I pretended I'd been to college, talked about Napier this and Napier that, and mentioned the library a lot too. He asked me what paper I read and I said the first name that came into my head.

I was praying he wouldn't ask about references, though I'd got two DIYs in my bag. So, I crossed my legs, oh so slowly, and he never mentioned them again. He told me to water one of his houseplants and it was covered in creepie-crawlies. I washed them off with warm soapy water like Mum used to do. I hope it'll survive, as I knocked a shoot off.

Lena said to watch out for shaky paws.

The old man phoned: 'I'm pleased to be able to advise you, Miss Whitadder, that you have secured the position advertised. Well done.'

Translation – I've got the job!

He's such a tiny old creature, I told Garry, not that he's interested. Like a wee, bent wrinkly leprechaun. I start tomorrow. I'm to get £15 an hour, 'if that is acceptable, Miss Whitadder?' That is acceptable, Sir Alexander. Miss Whitadder's so broke she'd take her clothes off for another fiver!

21st February

The Prof was in bed, hoarse, whispering me orders through his bluish lips. He'd a woolly hat on, his room like a fridge, and he told me to sit on the side of the bed. I hope there's nothing dodgy going on, surely to God he's too old for that kind of thing?

First job, he had me scrubbing some kind of pink stains on the floor. It looked like blood! Joiners were repairing his study window, taking down the board, and one of them (blondie) asked me if I was the old fellow's grand-daughter! He'd got the hots, trying to get my number, but I told him I was a lesbian to shut him up. What happened to the window? I looked in on the old man but he was fast asleep, yellow, snoring like a dog with his mouth wide open. Poor old bugger. To pass the time I made myself a coffee, looked at his books and pulled out some of the papers. At about one o' clock the polis chapped the door. I was petrified, thought maybe fat Al had sent them about the flood of IPA. But they just wanted to see the Prof. I told them he was ill in bed, too ill to talk, and they left unbothered, pronto.

After I'd finished, I walked around the loch, the geese stalking me and a couple of gulls dabbling themselves in the water. I'd like to live here, so would Garry. He'd love the birds, too. Mum phoned from the hospital, she'd had sandwiches again! I'll maybe try to get to see her tonight.

To celebrate I bought us an Indian for our tea.

22nd February

I tidied his clothes drawers for him. He's like an old-fashioned miser with a woollen sock heavy with cash, like a cosh. In amongst his tiny, grey vests, I found batteries (23), Bic pens (dozens of packets) and chocolate toffee eclairs. He gave me the sweets to take away, said he can't eat them anymore as they'd pull his 'stoppings' out. Why buy them, then? I said Garry liked them, and next thing I know he's slithering out of bed, slippers on, shuffling through to his lounge, tiptoeing round all the papers. He'd got a carrier bag of eclairs in his TV drawer and emptied them onto the floor for me to pick up, as if he was a king showering me with gold.

23d February

The Prof is up, in his stripy pyjamas and heavy dressing gown, and asked me to give him a lesson on his computer. He can type on it, but that's about all. Doesn't know even how to email. I showed him how to Google and he couldn't get over it, kept getting me to ask medical questions and was amazed at what he could find. 'In your hands, what a box of tricks it is!' he said. Then, 'No, a box of delights!' He repeated this endlessly. His cheeks looked as if someone had used a knife to play noughts and crosses on them, and the more he smiled, the more they bled. Nicks everywhere, including his earlobe. How? I asked him if he'd like me to shave him tomorrow and he nodded.

He wants to know how he can move stuff on the computer from one place to another, so, tomorrow, I'm going to show him how to copy and paste. Print, too. I whizzed about with the hoover but he told me to stop, he couldn't concentrate with the noise.

His bananas have all gone black in the cold.

24th February

A bunch of flowers greeted me. A really big one, yellow roses, must have cost him a fortune. He said I'd opened up new worlds for him, then he looked embarrassed. He'd tried 'the googling' on his own but he's forgotten how. So, I wrote it all out on a card for him (CAPITALS) and he seems to be able to follow it. He put his hand on my knee while we were sitting next to each other at the computer. I think it wasn't pervy, but I'll need to watch. Now I've become Jean but he's still 'Professor'. The milk in his fridge was sour again. No one had done his washing up, so I did. Garry and I went bowling.

3rd March

Opening a letter today, the old man went white as snow (cliché?), and almost collapsed before he got to his arm-chair. Annoyingly, muttering something like 'I'm off to my bed', he took it with him. What could it have said to do that to him? He's not won the lottery, that's for sure. Maybe it was from the doctor, the hospital, something like that? Big C? And I've only just got my toes under the table. If I get a chance I'll have a good look at it. From his bed, sitting up like a wee emperor in his bobble hat, he gave me instructions. I spent at least four hours going through files with him, putting the stuff (dry as dust) in date order, then I had to list the contents of two other bulging files and look out stuff from a folder he keeps by his bed.

The begonia is dead. Some wally has drowned it.

After lunch, he showed me his family book. He was almost coy, sheepish to begin with, saying maybe I wasn't interested, didn't have to look, didn't matter etc. but that he loved it, it always helped him in times of trouble. I hadn't a clue what he was talking about. Turns out he knows who all his relatives are – Generals, Sirs, other Professors, nobs of all sorts. His blood, as he put it. He knows what wedding presents his ancient relative received in 1693 ('Some silver, several rings, five guineas in a purse, and a pretty jewel set like a rose'). I took a photo. Some of the ancestors fought at Bannockburn, later, one was a Jacobite, another died at Culloden. Scots, though he doesn't sound it. One bit he read out loud, about his Mum, I think, made tears come to his eyes. Without thinking, I put an arm around him and gave him a wee cuddle. He's so skinny, his bones are like knives.

It made me think. I know nothing about me, a dog at Battersea would know more about itself. Tonight, at the hospital, I'm going to get anything I can from Mum and find out while I still can.

9 p.m.

Mum was fostered as a baby, then adopted by the foster-ers, my Gran and Grandpa. I'd sort of forgotten but I do remember her telling me years ago one Christmas, by the tree with the white and red flashing lights on. So, my Gran was no more related to me than that wee French bulldog. Thank God for that, she was one grumpy bitch. I'm going to go to Mum's flat and rifle around in her cupboard to see if we can find out anything about her. If we can find her address book we might be able to contact my Dad, but she thinks she's thrown it out. Like she did with him. I'll try online, too.

7th March

I found that letter today. No wonder he looked ill – scrawls of MURDERER, KILLER and other such. What the hell can he have done? Maybe it's to do with this blood case that he's so worried about, those victims in the papers. I heard one on Radio Forth, a mother, bad-mouthing all the doctors before starting to greet on air about her dead son. How the fuck could something like that have happened? There isn't a minute when he's not thinking, studying, preparing for this court case. Like it's an exam? He'll fry, 'cos he can't remember anything, repeats himself from minute to minute. Today he couldn't remember my name, called me Andrea, and that panicked him into a right shake. Anyway, I don't feel in peril even if he is a 'MURDERER, KILLER', he could be knocked over with a sneeze. Funny job, Lena doesn't believe what I tell her about it and no wonder.

She texted me, 'Child Minder 1 to Child Minder 2. Fancy a drink 2nite?'

Cheek.

In his kitchen cupboard, he had a tin (rusty) of lychees and I gave him some for lunch. Tried just the one myself – like a grey eyeball, slimy, but sweet and syrupy. While he was sleeping them off in his recliner, wrapped up in a green quilt, I looked through his photos, some coloured and a fair number in black and white. I found one of him, he looked like that Charlie Chaplin with masses of curly black hair and huge, dark eyes. Hard to put together that laughing face and the bony house elf, snoring, in the chair beside me. I'd have given him a second glance in the old days. I knocked over a vase of flowers, wetted a pile of his papers, but bundled them all into the bin before he woke up. Hope they don't matter! He's run out of his Omaprazole (?) and some blood-pressure pill. I'm to collect them from the chemist. When he woke he thought I was his MUM for a minute! Me and Garry went skating. He can go backwards now, that loopy, weaving way.

Mum slept all the time I was visiting and the Lady with the Bedpan looked daggers at me when I woke her to say goodbye. I just wanted a kiss, for fuck's sake.

13th March

Someone called Jimmy came and the Prof didn't seem very pleased to see him. He got that letter out and showed him, then they started muttering, they thought, in low voices together. I could hear it all, but I pretended I couldn't and kept on with my filing in the corner of the study.

Half the time they were talking about dull things, stuff like the Protein Fractionation Centre (?) but they always returned to the letter. They'd pick it up by a corner like mongooses as if it was a snake, glance at it, then the other would pick it up again. 'Ken' was another topic they picked away at – apparently, his memory's 'shot', join the club I thought. All the time the Prof was testing some rocky road I'd brought, with his teeth. Jimmy says biscuits, of any kind, make his teeth 'implode'. The few he's got left stand out like cactuses in a gulch.

'Who's she?' Jimmy asked, looking in my direction.

'The cat's mother,' the Prof replied. 'Meet . . .' (he had to think for a bit) '. . . Jean, my computer whizz stroke filing clerk cum domestic help.'

'Mmm. Margery wouldn't let me have one of them,' Jimmy says, smiling at me, revealing his stumps. Then he giggled: 'Mind, I might as well . . . with her dementia Margery's suspicious of everyone, today my hairdresser's in her crosshairs.'

'But you're bald as a coot,' the Prof said.

At that Jimmy just winked.

Funny, how I've got to like old-man speak. I never knew my Dad, out with the rubbish before I could walk. There's a gentleness about them, a whiff of charm. They treat me as if I'm a lady, unlike Cornford with his travelling hands.

Somehow, the Prof managed to tip his cup down his front. I'm going to take his washing home with me, no one seems to be doing it and it's all extra dosh. Felt a bit odd as I bundled up his Barbie-sized pants (no one could have a tinier bum), shirts and bedding. His trousers go to the cleaners, apparently, but I don't know who takes them. I told Lena that I'd got inside my boss's pants and she nearly choked on her crisps. He's got nothing in his fridge. How can his carers make his breakfast or his lunch? Should I ask him about his shopping?

16th March

Me and Garry went to see Mum. She's not coming out of hospital, told me that again herself, eyes closed, tired out with the pain. I remembered, just as we were leaving, to get her to write out her permission for me to see her adoption papers. I don't get it. She knows what it's for, but it could have been anything, a prescription, an Amazon parcel. Appeared to mean nothing. 'Doesn't she care who she is?' I whispered to Garry.

She heard, so my head was bitten off.

'If your "is" is only days, Jean, it doesn't much matter.'

But my 'is' should be a lot longer. I want to know who I am, everyone else does.

I asked her about Dad, but all she'd say was he was a split of the guitarist out of Slade, liked prawns and told her she looked like the Princess of Wales. Maybe that's where I got my way with words. Mind, as a librarian, I suspect her head was easily turned.

I want to go to Art College, art was all I was ever, really, any good at. I'm going to start drawing again, make a portfolio. I'll begin with life drawing. Could draw Garry, or the Prof when he's asleep in his chair, catching flies with his mouth. He'd be none the wiser. Could draw Mum, she's always asleep, motionless, like a still life. Still life. But at what fucking cost, they do nothing unless she's screaming in pain.

20th March

He got another of those letters. I spent most of my time mopping up his bathroom as he forgot he'd left one of the sink taps on. Thank God, he's not using the upstairs one as the ceiling would be down. He just rocked to and fro in his armchair, mumbling something. When he went for a rest I read the letter, took a photo of it on my phone to show Lena. Printed it from my computer too, here it is.

[printed copy stapled in]

Professor Anstruther

At last, the time for justice has come. While under your care, you infected me with AIDS, and let my brother die of it. We did not know what was in the Factor VIII, nor did our Mum, but you did. You knew. You are a criminal and,

soon, everyone will realise that. I want you to know that I can't wait to see you and your staff in the dock. I'll be there every day watching you. I've always believed that one day you would be exposed for what you did to us.
Sleep well.

Oliver Kurtz.

PS Remember me?

Jesus! No wonder he's so worried. Nothing would make him eat his lunch, not even his Pot of Joy. He's wasting away. I didn't sign up for any of this. I spent the evening with Lena as she's always up for a drink. Twenty shots between us. Then we went on to a drag show. 'Show us your tits!' she kept shouting, and Jinx did and that shut her up for a while as they were more impressive than hers. Looking at the queens, I felt that they were real and I was the fake. Lena says I should pack in my job 'cos the letter-writers might toss a firebomb through the letterbox or something. I said it's the ones that don't write to you first you need to worry about.

25th March
Come back call centre, all is forgiven! He had me working, non-stop, for hours on those papers of his. At one stage he waved a couple of sheets in front of my nose, saying all the while, 'Well, I never! Well, I never!'

Breaking my rule (if he starts, he's impossible to stop)

I asked him what the big deal was. He explained that the papers we'd been cataloguing showed that he'd tried to stop prisoners from donating their blood by 1983. Nearly my birthday year, I said, but he took no notice, rabbiting on about needle-sharing, homosexuals with the virus etc. 'Don't want them in the mix,' he said, spitting out a bit of his toast.

After lunch, I shaved him and he talks to me in the mirror like at the hairdresser's. Stares at me a bit too much for my liking, too, but closes his eyes if I catch him at it. He got me to cover his shaky paw while he attempted to sign some letters and papers. It jerks about all over the place. Eventually I said, why don't I do it? He laughed and said 'Go ahead', and my efforts were a lot better than his, or ours.

Just before I left, he shuffled into his bedroom and came out with a house key on a wee silk pillow.

'The Keys to the Kingdom, my Lady' he said. He trusts me. He gave me a blackened old teapot, candlesticks (???) and a condiment set as a present. God knows what I'll do with them, you'd think they were made of solid gold from the way he handled them. I think, in fact I know, he's fallen for me. No fool like one who falls for me.

1st April

Today I bundled him up, wrapped a scarf around his stringy, scraggy neck and we went for a walk, more like a shuffle, along the edge of the loch. I'd my arm through his, and several snails overtook us. The geese came waddling up, pecking around our feet, and I gave them some bread I'd taken from his bread-bin. We sat on a park bench, fed them, then shuffled on until I could hear him sucking in his breath. Maybe it was the cold air. Even with the ice at the edges, some daffs were still out, so I pinched some to put in a vase when we got back. We must have looked an odd sight, him and me, because I almost had to pull him about, a bit like a reluctant, wrinkly toddler. He'd a permanent drip on his nose and his lips turned a new shade of blue. But when I helped him back into his chair, he sighed, pressed my hand and said it'd been a lovely outing.

While he snored away under his quilt, I looked in his fridge in the kitchen as I was starving, but there was only ancient green, mouldy cheese and a polythene bag of old, soft tomatoes, plus some out-of-date yoghurts. Threw the lot out. No wonder he's skin and bones. I left him and went to the Co-op and got us both sandwiches. Then I looked at his book again.

'Mary Stewart (Ardmore) (c.1559–1593)

She was the third daughter of John Stewart, 4th Earl of Ardmore.

1573: In this year, on 18th November, she married Sir Duncan Halkirk and had eleven children. At the time of her marriage she was about fifteen years of age.

1593: Her father, the 4th Earl, was Lord High Chancellor of Scotland in 1578. He was a zealous catholic and strongly opposed the Reformation in 1560. With the

Earls of Moray and Moreton, he defeated Huntly and his Gordons at Corrichie in 1562. He entertained Queen Mary in the Ardmore Forest. He is reputed to have died of poison administered by Moreton in April 1557. Mary Stewart's mother was believed to have the power of incantation, and at the birth of James VI cast the pain from Queen Mary into Lady Rires.'

He's descended from a witch! And not just any old one, one who looked after the Royals. Handy trick that, inflicting labour pains on others. I teased him about following in the family tradition by becoming a witchdoctor, but he didn't laugh. He liked the tuna and cucumber, wolfed it down, but never offered to pay me. Suppose he thought I'd made it from his stuff.

Drew the old man in his chair. 'Dobby at rest', I'm calling it.

Saw Mum and told her I'd made an appointment at the Adoption Unit of the National Records Office. She's so pale, on oxygen and hardly looked up when I came in, just squeezed my hand. The nurses seem to just leave her sandwiches in front of her and then take them away on a trolley. I tried to give her some jelly but she closed her mouth like a trap, wouldn't let the spoon in. Ice cream, no better. Her chart says 'eating as normal'. 'A work of fiction,' I said to the uniformed trolley-dolly as she rattled past.

Funny, sitting beside Mum's bed, I looked at her profile and I could see a clear family resemblance to Gran. How come? They both have that near meeting of nose and chin, Punch-like, and bright little eyes. I have Mum's hands, too, long fingers, but not her legs. I'm all leg, stilts like a crane.

Let her live.

While I was brushing her hair, Nurse Ratchet shooed me away (before closing time), said I was tiring Mum out.

4th April

Had a bit of a heavy night last night, celebrating Lena's thirty-third and it was an effort not to throw up this morning. Garry moaned I woke him up coming in. The Prof, first thing, having told me that I looked a bit peely-wally, moved into doctor mode and told me I must drink a lot (ha ha), and I said, no worries, I had been. Actually, unknown to him I did throw up in his basin, but cleaned it up with toilet paper. We did some copying and pasting onto some kind of fact sheet that he's obsessed with preparing, it's got a timeline with events marked against them. Just talking exhausted him today, he hadn't the energy to put on his slippers, so I put them on him. He remarked that I was his handmaid, or, rather, footmaid.

An old woman, Eileen something, came with her fat, aggressive daughter, Bee. They were no sooner through the door, than Bee demanded tea for them both, which I made. As the old folk were chattering together in the lounge, she pulled her finger along a couple of picture frames, examined the dust and wrinkled her nose at me whilst beckoning with a crooked, dusty finger. I'm not her employee.

'Isn't this your job?'

'If he asks.'

'He may not always think to ask.'

That threw me. I do some stuff on my own, his washing and so on, and he keeps me busy. Seeing me on the floor, the Sumo wrestler jumped in for the kill.

'If not cleaning, what do you do?'

'I file, catalogue, precis, print . . . I help with all this paperwork and stuff.'

'Well, my dear, I suspect you'd be more use to him if you spent less time on that and more on dusting, hoovering, washing the floors and so on. The domestic duties.'

Patronising cow. Speechless, I went into the kitchen, made her another cup of tea and then spat in it. She drank it, thankfully, and I was tempted to offer her a third. He is not all there always, I know that, but we get along just fine.

11th April

There was a mass of plukes on the Prof's face this a.m., 'shingle' spots, he says. They're all around his eye, across his cheek and around his mouth. I shaved him as best as I could, felt his forehead and it was on fire. Burning up. I hope I don't catch it, pass it on to Garry. With him complaining, saying he was fine really, I sent him off to bed and, in minutes, I saw his little head sticking out above the covers. I think he needs someone to order him to slow down, relax, get well. Like with Mum.

Eyes shut, he protests that he's got 'too much to do'??

Why does he bother? He's just muddling himself – worse, scaring himself. Sometimes, when I read a letter, say, I used to ask him about someone in it or what something means, but he had no more clue than me, got agitated, tetchy about it. But he's got all these papers everywhere, and it's superstition, like touching wood, for him. He imagines that having had them through his hands, on his skin, smelling them, will save him. I help, but that won't.

I whiled away my time, reading his books and stuff. Then I texted Lena the name of tonight's club, washed the floor and got him some yoghurt. He said it was sour, 'inedible' but refused to eat anything else. Later today I have my appointment at the Records place.

6 p.m.

The Registrar (think the lovechild of Marge Simpson and Shrek) met me, sat me down in a side room, apologised, and said that due to a flood a number of their records had suffered damage in the cold winter of 1964, with pipes bursting and so on. Everything had been improved since, humidifiers and so on. Fifty years ago? You might hope so.

Unfortunately, the certificate I was looking for, she said, was amongst those damaged. Shit. The petition (?) had been destroyed, the adoption report damaged and much of the birth certificate stained, but she had a digest of the information that it had been possible to obtain from the remaining legible documents. I could get a photocopy of them, if I liked. Why would I do that? I took a photo of them all with my phone and it's not that bad. She handed over a copy of the digest sheet, and I took it anyway. But you can make out pretty well everything from the certificate, it's just watery, smudged. With the way she spoke, low, whispering, suggesting I speak to a counsellor if I wanted, I expected I'd get nothing. But it's fine, just fine. Mum was born in some hospital, I can't remember the name but it's in the photo, in Dingwall in 1962. The digest gives her birth mother's name as Isabel Euphemia Faulkner and her Dad was Michael Ignatius Faulkner. He's down as a 'Musician'. Could My Gran have been some kind of rock chick? I could get into this.

14th April

Surprise! No miracles performed by the ear people, so he still can't hear what I say and buzzes about, bumping into things, like an angry (deaf) little hornet. He was curled up asleep in his recliner (that purple bobble hat pulled down over his eyes) by the time I got here, and too knackered to do any paperwork but he assures me that GREAT THINGS had been achieved that afternoon between him and Eileen. I asked how Bee was, and he said she'd been peaky with a stomach upset but was now fully recovered. 'Bossy bint,' I said below my breath but, by magic, he caught that one and said 'Quite'. He asked how I was getting on with my researches and I said I'd found my Gran's and Grandad's name and the name of the place where Mum was born in 1962. I'm going to see it. He says it feels different, walking the streets you know your people walked, you see the places with new eyes. I like that idea.

15th April

I met 'Rough Andrea' as he calls her. He asked me to ping some of his pills out of their blister packs (his fingers won't work to get them out of the plastic) and put them into a spare brown bottle. There I am sitting on his bed, listening to Lana Del Rey on my phone, pinging the pills and minding my own business. In sweeps the Ginger Giant as if she owns the place, sees me and freezes like she's spotted a cockroach scuttling across the floor or something.

'What are you doing there?' she demands.

'Helping the Prof with his pills.'

'You've no right,' Ginger says, red-faced, 'I'll need to tell the office.'

No 'Hi', 'Hello', 'Good morning', 'Pleased to meet you', nothing. I had every right. 'Away back to the circus with you,' I reply, continuing my pinging, 'the other clowns are lonely.'

First Bee, now her. What's wrong with these people?

16th April

Took a bus and shoogled the whole road to Inverness, then on to Dingwall on a damp seat. After speaking to a couple of Poles and one Weegie, I got directions to 'St Gerard's'. It's behind a wall, an old place, big, with a huge garden that leads down to the firth. I asked someone in a nearby Greggs if it had been a hospital but she said no, a reformatory, then the Scripture Union had it for a while until someone bought it and its been a B and B for a long time. I took a photo to show Mum and Garry. The heel came off my shoe so I hobbled the streets, difficult on cobbles too.

24th April

I knew it. Sure enough, he thinks Garry's my child. He's bought an expensive train set to give him and had, God knows how, wrapped it up himself. I just took it. Easier this way. Far too late to tell him now.

25th April

Was he a monster? He needed me to copy and paste something from the Inquiry site onto a Word doc and I did it, but I read it too. This is the second one saying the same thing. Did he, really, let people go on taking stuff that he KNEW was polluted with the AIDS virus? Who would do that? Really? Who? I thought the letter-writers were nuts, but, maybe, they're not? I didn't say anything but he must have seen my expression. He looked me in the eyes, started gibbering, whining, explaining and, all the time, tears were rolling down his wee monkey face. My first thought was that if Harry was my son, I'd kill him, not just send him those letters. But I couldn't bear to see him, trembling, head bowed, almost hysterical. So I followed my gut, went up to him and hugged his bony shell and I could feel him relax, recover and unwind. He's just an old, old man now, no more than that, whatever he may once have been. Now, you could call him crabbit, fussy, weird, all sorts of things . . . but he'd never be that bad, do that. Would he? No. So, they are the fruitcakes. No wonder he's like a headless chicken worrying about this Inquiry, it must be as welcome as sick on a birthday cake.

I left him in bed with his nose in his Family Book, rheumy-eyed but cheering himself up with his ancestors. They're amazing, better than Red Bull or weed for him. Cheaper too. I could do with some of those!

At teatime, that Bee woman called with his coat and umbrella. I took them off her at the door. When I didn't invite her in, she looked miffed, almost tried to peer round the door, withdrawing her foot only as I eyed her. She's not running free in here again with her rude finger.

'He's indisposed,' I said through the door, 'certainly too ill to see you.'

The only Isabel Euphemia, born in 1962 and got off the net, says that she was born in Rosedean Hospital, Inverness. Her mother was Laura Harrower and her father's name was Allan Archibald Anstruther (Architect). What are the odds? Isabel Anstruther. Lots of them, Anstruthers, about, probably, so I'm not saying a word to him yet. Need to let Mum know first, if she can take it in. Fingers crossed, though, I'm going to flower on the tree. Sent a text to Lena ordering her to curtsey when she next sees me.

I told the Prof, once he was calmer and drinking his

coffee, that Garry was over the moon with his train. Well, what else could I say? He'd left the price on and it cost him seventy-five pounds! More than my week's wage. I'll flog it on e-bay. But maybe, one day, we'll be travelling on the Orient Express.

When I was in the kitchen wiping up some orange gunge he'd spilled on the fridge and the cooker, I heard a scratching, scrabbling noise behind the plaster like lots of tiny claws. If he's got rats I'm leaving.

FIFTH NARRATIVE *by* ANTHONY SPARROW

Past eleven o' clock at night and I was still reading, but my eyes were beginning to close. I put the notebook down. Apart from being tired, having earlier that same day catalogued Anstruther's collection of children's books in the upstairs nursery, I found myself unexpectedly dis appointed. Jean Whitadder (murderess that she was) had seemed to have some spark about her, a roguish Becky Sharpe/Artful Dodger-like quality, unrepentant, and in thrall to nobody. Now she was exposing herself as all too workaday, all too mundane in her aspirations, drearily quotidian in her dreams. To wish to claim common an cestry with her employer, Professor Sir Alexander Anstruther! And why, pray? All because the man had a pedigree that might have come from a Scots *Almanac de Gotha*. Well, in my book, Not Good Enough. I suppose she knew nothing of poor old Anna Anderson (who believed herself to be the Grand Duchess Anastasia) and spent the bulk of her life in nursing homes, sanitoria and asylums due to similar, albeit more grandiose, delusions? Did such a fate await her? That she should be subject to such a commonplace one almost made me toss her scribblings into the fire. What is this pathological urge to 'raise' one's status, attach oneself to the blue-blooded, the titled? Such a poor example was set by Ms Markle, as I shall continue to call her. Frankly, I find it pathetic, pathetic and demeaning. I am no communist but I bend the knee to no one, unless a book (purchase or sale) depends upon it. Surely this generation would prefer to be descended from Victoria and David than Victoria and Albert? Has *Hello* achieved nothing? That *Downton Abbey* class-porn peddled by Mr Fellowes has a lot to answer for.

And, of course, Anstruther is a place in Fife, a small coastal village less than five miles from my own exalted premises. In Crail, the very fishmonger's shop is called 'Anstruthers'. I, myself, know two other Anstruthers, and one of those is an Allan Anstruther. A gravedigger by profession, as it happens, with a heavy skunk habit and not an inch of pelt free from tattoos. One of his arms is decorated with the insignia of Rangers' Unionism, and its twin sports an Independence saltire. Plainly, a conflicted soul (and body). Would she believe herself to be his long-lost daughter? I doubt it.

The other is an abattoir worker. So, spoilt for choice.

An unattractive Dutch Sparrow with sideburns, too much phlegm in his mouth (such an ugly language) and genealogical pretensions called on me once, but, he, too, was more of a cuckoo.

'You and I are fourth cousins once removed.'

'Me, Mr Blobby and Prince Charles,' I said, as loftily as my lisp would allow, 'and every other inhabitant of these green and pleasant lands.'

Really!

In the world of Rare Books, provenance is all. It is not enough to believe that this copy of *On the Origin of Species* belonged to Mr Charles Darwin himself; if that is to be established it will be in consequence of an examination of the bindings, the paper, the marginalia, book plates, book rhymes and inscriptions. Hard evidence is required. I am ever vigilant for fakes.

Poor old Jean has next to nothing, little more than fresh air.

Anthony Sparrow

ADDENDUM

The day after I wrote the above, I went to an auction in Edinburgh. I muscled my way into a seat at the front, nearly tripping over a thoughtless punter's golf umbrella, and took the grubby little notebook from the pocket of my blazer. I had five minutes to kill before my first lot. Suffice it to say, in the next hour, for the first time ever, I missed everything; saw no one wiggle a finger, nod a head or signal with a rolled-up catalogue to the auctioneer. I didn't even hear his gavel strike the rostrum. My head remained down, my whole being concentrating on the woman's words, hypnotised by them. Thus, I missed the two oddities I had come for; an 1850 edition of *Holleck's Diseases of Women* and the only known edition of Winter's *Trichologia*. A disaster, as I had promised them to someone I wished to keep in with, needed to keep in with if one looks to the long term as I do. So be it. That superannuated gynaecologist will simply have to wait. How would I explain the matter to her? The truth is that all my attention was taken by Jean Whitadder's words, but, perhaps, I got stuck in a traffic jam, awoke with a fever, swallowed a fly? The trick, I find, is to believe your own story.

JEAN WHITADDER'S NOTEBOOK
[continued]

28th April
I got a £500 bonus today.

30th April
Tiny, but a slave-driver, nonetheless. I'm back on his 'line'. As usual, in between typing, I read the stuff round about. His great, great, great, great grandfather was the first man in all Scotland to introduce the cultivation of neeps. Pity he bothered, I say. In 1773 neeps were, 'still such a rarity that they were served as dessert in Edinburgh dinner parties'. With a haggis custard, I expect. Another ancient relative, in 1653, 'while fighting on the slopes of Ben Nevis, with some of General Monck's troops . . . killed an English soldier by biting out his throat.'

Now, that's my boy!

More importantly, in between typing out his stuff I managed to find the bit I'm interested in. His sister was called 'Isabel Euphemia' (!!!!!) and as I was just about to turn the pages to find their dad's name, the phone rang and I had to answer it, then hand it over to him. While he was gabbing, that toxic cow, Bee, showed herself in, lumbered over and exiled me to the kitchen. I looked at him pleadingly, but, receiver in hand, he nodded. Jesus Christ, how long will I have to wait!

As my time was up and Bee was still hogging him, I made myself scarce. Later, I bumped into him again. As I was going into the supermarket, he was being hauled, roughly, out of it. He was sort of squealing, muddy too, from a fall, I suppose. People were looking, mouths open, and I recognised the man pulling him about. It was that shit, Garry. I screamed at him to let the old man go and he did, looking daggers at me, then shouting something rude at the old fellow. I took his bag off his arm, manhandled him, slowly, slowly, back home. He was so knackered I just helped him off with his trousers and put him into his bed. Then I looked for the Hot Chocolate but couldn't find it, so gave him a hot cup of soup instead. He mumbled that 'He wasn't a thief'. Pathetic, an old man like that, less memory left than a goldfish. Shoplifting! He'd only a tin of prunes and a Twix in his bag! Garry's not a security man, he's a fucking professional bully, more like. He enjoys that job far too much, relishes 'catching people at it', most, probably, poor (literally) sods, or demented old folk. 'On a bonus, are you?' I asked. Any shoplifter worth his salt would have little difficulty in outwitting him. If he ever handled me the way he was handling the Prof, he'd get a kick in the balls. I need to shop around a bit myself, I think. The old man kept on thanking me, saying I was his guardian angel, that he didn't know what he'd do without me, I'd saved him etc.

By his bedside was a family photograph, him, his sister and their parents. I picked it up and looked really properly at it this time. As ever, he looks like Charlie Chaplin, but beside him stands the doppelganger of my Mum. 'Isabel, my sister, aged about nineteen,' he said, sleepily, 'in her prime.' I hadn't noticed it before.

Like my Mum, he needs me.

4th May

I tried to ask him about his sister but he said he wouldn't talk today, if I didn't mind, as his jaw hurt. The book I need was right by his bed. I put some old cream I found in a bathroom cupboard upstairs on the side of his face. I gave him coffee, too, which he drank through a straw. Then I left, as I'd nothing to do except deliver an envelope for him. He said there was a bonus in it for me if I did. I sealed the envelope, put a stamp on it and took it to George Street.

I must see that book.

5th May

He's in a frenzy, keeps saying that he can't think, remember, what he thought THEN because of what he knows NOW. Despite everything we've done, I don't think he knows anything much now. He was also as jittery as hell, hands like mad little birds fluttering their wings in amongst all the papers. Sometimes I think he's talking rubbish, real rubbish, can't possibly read all the stuff that is going through his hands, never mind retain much of it. If I'd a tranquilliser I'd slip him one in his juice, or dart him, as he's like an overwound clock; hands spinning round the face and the alarm zinging too. Should I get a doctor? He is a bloody doctor, he spat at me. By his bed was an envelope with a letter hanging half out of it. I read it in the kitchen. It was just a sheet of names – murderer, evil bastard, swine, shit and so on with an illustration of a hangman's noose and the question 'Go on, why don't you?' No wonder he's in such a state. I answered his phone and it was Bee asking for him on her Mum's behalf to discuss 'Statistics'. No, I said, nope, nah, no way. He's in no condition to talk about anything.

'I beg your pardon?'

'Granted.'

Just as I sensed she was about to put the phone down on me, I did it on her. Sweet.

Those spots seem better but his face is still tender to shave after the fall. Garry's complaining that I spend too much time here. Jealous git. Where has the Prof put that book?

6th May

Finally, I managed to remember how to get a copy of Allan Archibald Anstruther's birth certificate on the net. His father is (Col.) Archibald Rannoch Anstruther, his mother is Katherine Isabella Gordon. His wife, Laura Harrower's mother, is Helen Anne Livingston Rose and her father is

Sir James Harrower, a Surgeon. They sound like nobs?

The Prof phoned to say not to come, he sounded worse than usual but was insistent, saying that he was going out himself and would have nothing for me to do today. Will he be alright?

8th May

Garry and me took the day off. We stayed in bed till after 12 and then went to Ocean Terminal, he tried to get me a ring (!), but I wasn't having any of that. I told him he'd do in the meanwhile and he laughed, thought I was joking, taking the piss. I'm not. He's always looking round, checking up on me to see if I'm smiling at someone else or 'flirting' as he calls it. I'm not putting up with that crap again. Accused me of fancying the turnip driving the bus. 'Bang on,' I said, looking him straight in the eye and licking my lips. I'd be wearing a burkah if he had his way. Hacked off, I added 'Marry you? You're a bastard, you hurt old men like the Prof.'

'Gents like him think they can get away with it . . . don't have to pay in life, I show 'em they do,' he says, unbothered, finishing his Magnum, with choc dribbling down off his chin and onto his T-shirt.

Then it hit me.

'You knew who he was, didn't you?'

'Course I did.'

'Did it anyway?'

'Oh no, doll, did it because . . .' He nods, grinning.

Later, when I said I needed to see Mum, he went in the

huff and wouldn't say a word the rest of the way on the bus. I reminded him that she was DYING. He was still in one when we got off, so I said he could get lost, I'd had enough of him, was going for chips after the hospital and by the time I got back he should have packed his crap and fucked off out of my life. This status update is long overdue.

Mum is dying.

10th May

Garry's gone. How do I always manage to pick one tosser after another? Maybe I get carried away by the shiny wrappers, forget that what's inside may not be good for me. There should be a health warning on him – 'Garry harms you and others around you' or 'Garry causes ageing of the skin'.

14th May

I let myself in to the Prof's house at about 2 p.m. but he was at the Eye Hospital. He'd left a note asking me to go through some more documents, put them in date order, number them and list them. I meant to do that first, but I couldn't concentrate on anything and, instead, ransacked his house trying to find that book. It was under his bed in amongst several polythene bags of letters. One was marked 'Isabel'.

We are related. His sister, Isabel Faulkner, is my real, birth Gran. I can hardly type the words.

My Mum's real name was Camilla Faulkner.

I am an heiress, surely to God? This is, could be, life-changing stuff; no more Niddrie, Own Brand, Pound Shop, roll-your-own shit!

I know who I am.

All the numbered (40) genealogical trees end with Alexander Anstruther and Isabel Anstruther, so I still know nothing about her. But I belong. I am, to myself, SOMEBODY. I've not disappeared up my own arse, it just gives me, my life, a meaning it was missing. Funny, I didn't know it was, but now it's here, I can feel it. I am who I was yesterday but I have more of a place in time, those before me are real, concrete. Me, myself, am more solid.

Those celebs on *Who Do You Think You Are* sometimes bawl on finding stuff out (Gt Gt Granny pegs it in the workhouse or whatever), and I used to think they were putting it on for the camera. But I understand it now. I don't know these people but they are MY people. If they'd all been criminals, coal miners, circus trapeze artists they'd be just as much mine too. Roots, as they say. Not fussy what they are, just need some.

This changes everything.

When the Prof got back, he was bent, grey, knackered. Watching him through the window, he almost fell out of the taxi, the driver caught him, and now he's no energy left for anything. While he was breathless in bed, I went to the supermarket and got him a ready meal for tonight and some lilies. He's my Great Uncle! HE, PROFESSOR SIR ALEXANDER ANSTRUTHER, IS MY GREAT UNCLE. I almost shouted it out loud in Tesco's.

I tried to say something to him, couldn't stop myself, but he couldn't keep his eyes open, take anything much in, and when I tell him I want him to understand, to believe me, to see that it's all true.

I must be disciplined, choose my time.

Garry left another message on my phone again, said he'd gone to meet me at the Prof's house, wanted to talk, say he was sorry, blah, blah. I'm glad I wasn't there, I'm not listening to that shite again. He's controlling, but his reign is over. Where the hell did he get the address from, I wonder? I told the Prof I was going to take some letters home with me, to number, date etc. and I murmured they were marked Isabel. At first he protested, in a hoarse little voice, saying they'd nothing to do with the Inquiry etc., but I said they'd still need doing and he didn't reply, so I just took them. In a way, they're mine, anyway. I went to see Mum and tell her my news, but I don't think what I said meant anything to her. Her puffy, pastry-coloured face was covered by an oxygen mask again, she looked quite out of it with her eyes rolling upwards, moaning, and I'm not sure how much she could hear. The machines were bleeping and so on. I wished I was dead. Ratchet came after about five minutes, said 'Mum' had had a bad day, feverish most of the time. Suggested I 'for pity's sake, leave her in peace' as there was 'nothing I could do'. You don't say. They're giving her antibiotics to try and bring her temperature down, but if that doesn't work, well, there's nothing else. I was too tired for anything after that, wept in the bus. She's only fifty-one. Fucking, fucking, fucking cancer.

She is all I have.

15th May

The Prof was away all day at the Inquiry and that Andrea's supposed to be there for his tea and bath. I did a little light housework, one in the eye for Bee, then I turned to the letters.

Oh, how I like my Gran! In the poly bag, there were some letters from her to the Prof when she was just little (with scribbly pictures) and he was at University, in 1950. Lots from when she was sent away to school and he'd begun working in hospitals and some from her at Art College. There's a huge seventeen-year gap between them. I wonder why? Carbon copy letters from him mixed in, too, and a few from their Mum, MY great Gran. I fit now, I have a place. My life is not just mine, it's theirs too, as theirs is mine. I will do something with myself, with my life. I like her voice, I like her views, I like her and she is mine. All children, I suppose, think they've come from somewhere else, somewhere more exotic, gold-plated. I certainly hoped that, looking at my Gran with her down-turned barcode pucker-mouth, and barbed tongue. She never liked me, said I was 'too clever by half', 'too quick for my own good' etc. She wasn't all bad, but apart from their shared weakness for Daniel O'Donnell, Mum and her had nothing in common. Grandpa could take money out of my ears, I remember that, but he died before I was seven. Oh, and he seemed to have an endless supply of creme eggs.

16th May

The Prof was too ill to go to the Inquiry today. He never got out of bed and I brushed his hair, tried to make him comfortable, as he was so weak, lifeless. He was confused, too hot, seemed concerned about his hairbrushes. I stayed with him until late, trying, and failing, to get him to take some soup and cheesy biscuits. Threw out the rotten, smelly fish. He's so weak he doesn't even want to listen to the radio. I sketched him asleep, then read more of his stuff until it got dark and, finally, can you bloody believe it, that stupid plonker Garry came when I'd gone to get my coat. I heard a high, terrified scream, and I rushed into the Prof's room and found Garry peering in the window, face pressed right up against the pane, freaking the poor old man out. He looked like a nutcase, Christ knows who the Prof thought he was. Maybe one of those 'Murderer' let-ter-writers or something? I tried to calm him, soothe him, told him there was nobody there, and then I marched out and told that stupid plonker, Garry, to fucking SCRAM.

'But we need to talk, babes.'

'There's nothing to say . . . except it's not me, it's you. Clear enough?'

'I'm not giving up, I'll be back.'

'Nope, my lines. I'm the Terminator.'

Inside again, the old fellow kept asking me who it was, but I could hardly admit to the old man it was Garry, my 'little boy'. Garry's got form stalking people, like that time he haunted me, nicked my key and rearranged things in my flat just to freak me out. Worked, too. Weirdo.

When should I tell the Prof?

I really want him to meet Mum. It's unbearable, I know so much, they so little. Neither have a closer relative upon this earth, apart from me. I want to share it with them. What will they make of each other? I will be their interpreter. What will Mum think when she hears that Professor Sir Alexander Anstruther is her uncle? Bet it'll mean next to nothing, never would have. She has all the curiosity of a sheep. My darling, darling sheep.

I must choose my time, but she may have little left.

20th May

Funny day. One of the letters I was cataloguing came from the Prof's lover, and he's a man. Who would have thought? Can't picture him with a man any more than I can a soup sandwich. I catalogued it, in the way he'd shown me, but I could tell he was pissed off from the look he threw me when he checked the index. What was I supposed to do? Ignore it? Classify it under 'The Blood Transfusion Service'? If he didn't want me to see it, he should have fished the thing out of the pile before I got it. As if anyone nowadays gives a toss, including me. His house has no nice stuff, leather, fur, nothing much matches. Maybe he's not very gay? After all, he wears a bobble hat inside. I wonder if there are any other love letters in the piles? Hope so.

When I was in the bathroom, I accidently tipped a

mug of water off the hand basin and onto his vinyl floor. I opened his cupboard, below the sink, to get a cloth and about thirty electric razors fell out. He's got a powerpoint but he's not using it, just buying a new razor every time the battery's gone flat. If no batteries, he uses that brush and razor. In the cupboard were a couple of pairs of his dolly pants, a fork and two black bananas. If he hadn't been huffy with me, I'd have shown him how to charge things up. While I was busy trying to stuff things back in, the phone went. It was Bee, so I put it down saying 'The Clap Clinic is now closed'.

Just as I was about to bring THE SUBJECT up, that arsehole, Garry, haunted us again. Face flattened on the glass. I looked straight through him. Then I went upstairs, opened the window and emptied the contents of the food bin on him, baked beans and all.

At home, that evening, I read this letter from MY Gran to the Prof:

8th June 1962
14 Chalcott Square,
London

Darling Alex,

Thank you for your letter. I am so ashamed, so sorry for what has happened and for biting your head off on Tuesday. You are right, I am pregnant and I should not have lied to you (should have known better!!). The father is another student at Goldsmiths, he's into life-drawing too and we went to a party and between the Pimms, smoochy music and someone's joint, well, you can imagine. Andrew's a post-grad Yank, from Washington DC, and, what's worse, married already with two kids. He's going back to the States in 'the Fall' as he calls it. Mummy and Daddy have no idea about any of this so, please, please, please do not tell them. Promise me? I cannot bear to be the one that lets them down, embarrasses them in front of family and friends. They'd never say it but I'd be the 'first' and in an unrelievedly bad way. We don't do 'Bastards' do we? Anyway, it's all in hand. I plan to have an abortion and Andrew has fixed it up for me somewhere in Soho. Celia is the only other person who knows and she's going to go to the clinic with me. She's had an abortion herself and says it's no big deal at all, you're not even kept in overnight. At the moment, I feel fine most of the time and haven't had any morning sickness or anything. So, please don't worry about me, I have everything in hand and I know exactly what to do. Think no more about it and I'll soon get my head around it, I know.

Just so you know, Mummy told me on the phone that they're going on holiday, first to Brora, fishing somewhere or other, and then on to Perugia to stay with the Grand Old Man. Dad's got some RIBA chief for a couple of days and plans to have you to dinner to help out with him. I think he's hoping you'll bring Trish with you to leaven the pudding.

By the way, did they accept your article on Type 3 Von Willebrands (?) and pregnancy? That they should be so lucky, I say. See you, I hope, at Cousin Hugh's birthday tea and please bring, if you've got a minute, that book you were talking about, the one about the spy/hoover salesman in Havana by G. Greene. If I'm allowed to borrow it? I'm going to hitch home with Celia, a couple of nights before.

All love,
Isabel.

22nd May

Mum died, face red, contorted, gasping, rattling, as I held her hand. It was grotesque, beyond my worst imagination, and time stood still, seconds passing like years as I willed her to go, just go. The gin I'd taken with me in my bag eventually knocked me out until I was sick on the hospital bed, came to with her cold hand in mine. My head feels as if it's made of glass and might shatter at any second. No one really knows me or loves me anymore. Without her, I'm alone. And she never knew. I said No Way at the hospital when the Doctor asked for her corneas and heart valves. Sod the vultures. I don't want her cut up, butchered like a bit of meat. It's not her but it's all that's left of her. I saw her later, but it didn't look like her any more, white skin, face caved in, didn't smell like her and I can't get that smell out of my nose. A pot-bellied Reverend hovered about the place, wanting 'to pray' with me, until I swatted him away. I knew this was going to happen, have known for weeks, but I didn't expect I'd feel so empty, so lost. Better for her, though, a million times. No pain, peace at last.

24th May
Found a typed carbon from the Prof in amongst Isabel's letters to him.

10th June 1962
13 Dean Street
Edinburgh

My darling Isabel,

I got your letter of 8th inst. Please let me, as your much older (and wiser?) brother, have my say. You are the one who is pregnant and it is your choice and your choice alone. Be in no doubt, I recognise that fact and respect it. However, as a medical man, I have, obviously, seen much more of terminations, and their physical and mental effects (both in the long term and short term) than you have.

Equally as important, I have known you from the moment you arrived upon this earth. Thanks to you I became acquainted with rats, rabbits, gerbils, cats, bantams and dogs. Did you know that Ma and Pa only got Brandy because you tormented them, bullying and begging for a dog for over a month? You tried to save that broken-winged gull, fed those orphan hedgehogs and re-homed that foul, vicious bull terrier whose scars on my shins I bear to this day. Throughout my childhood there were never any animals at home until you arrived and started exerting your IRON will. What I am trying to get across is that I know you, you love life, life in all of its forms from wasps upwards. Do you remember how upset you were by those rabbits with myxy? You tried to cure them, bathed their eyes? Even in London you have a budgie and Ma tells me you had/have plans for a kitten.

I do not think there are many, if any, women who undergo a termination and then never think about it again. The majority get on with their lives but, at the back of their mind, remains the child who never was. Would it have been a girl, would she have had blue eyes, how old would she be now? A few, and I am convinced you would be one of them, find life difficult to bear in the light of what they have done. They do not forget it or forgive themselves. Some develop depression or worse, need treatment.

I do understand your situation. I would not advise you to marry your Yank even if you could. He's two-timed his wife and I do not like (or recommend to you) those who deceive their nearest and dearest in that way. You could, however, borrow his name later, if need be. So, marriage is out. But termination is not your only option. You could have the baby and damn everyone who disapproves. Ma and Pa would come around eventually (Granny might take that little bit longer) and how could any of them fail to love any child of yours? Our blood. You are only twenty-one, the bud of life unfurling its petals, and you may feel you are not yet ready for a child, could not cope with a baby. But, remember, I can help. I am a consultant already and very well remunerated. I have no dependents, no intention of acquiring any (whatever Trish may imagine!) and live a remarkably frugal, but content, existence. I could easily support you and your child. We could get a nanny, you could transfer to Edinburgh Art College and, bingo, everything's sorted!

If, for whatever reason, that suggestion does not meet with your approval (and it does meet with mine, I promise – I would love it. Honestly, I would love a little niece or nephew), then the remaining option, in my view, is adoption. It's not the course I think you should pursue (unlike the last one), but it is still preferable to termination. We could find you somewhere out of the way (John o' Groats or Land's End) you could have your baby and then hand it over to an agency. Your life could continue much as before, the baby would have a good home and no one would be any the wiser about anything. Please, Izzy, think about what I am saying?

I have no religious objection to termination and it is your body. But, I'm convinced you would always regret what you had done and you don't have to do it. My offer is real and if you chose not accept it then I will understand, but, please, consider adoption in such circumstances? Or else, best of all, come and stay with me and we'll look after the baby together.

Much love,
Alex

P.S. You can borrow *Our Man in Havana*. Can I borrow *A Burnt-Out Case*?

If she was here I could have shown her, shared all this with her. Her Mum, her Uncle. Too late for all that now, but, God, how I wish she'd known. He saved us both.

The Chinese lady undertaker suggested 'Mumma' be cremated in her smartest work suit, black with a blue trim, and she'd dress her. What a thought. I got it to them from the cleaners just before they closed for the night. One of her librarian pals (Dot?) phoned, weepy, to say she wouldn't make the funeral but would send a wreath. The Crematorium want to know what music, so I suggested Sinatra. Mum loved 'My Way' and 'They Shoot Horses Don't They', but I couldn't remember who sang that. No address and no Daniel, I couldn't face it. No wake either. She'd not care and I don't want to be handing out Cheesy Whatsits to a bunch of strangers. The Chinese lady frowned, maybe they take a cut on the catering? Got Zombie pills from Lena to help me sleep.

27th May

Mum's Funeral. Too tired to write.

30th May

The Prof phoned and I promised to go tomorrow evening.

1st June

I don't know where to begin. Maybe I'll try for chrono-logical order, if I can stick to it. I let myself in and he was in bed, the light low, and in the shadows he appeared, more than ever like a little yellow elf, his bobble-hatted head sticking up above the white bed-sheets. At first, he seemed cross, annoyed that I'd not come before, peevish with me, and kept not looking me in the eye. Bit too like bloody Garry, actually. So, crying by then, I explained that Mum had died and that I'd had to arrange the funeral etc. and apologised for having to neglect him and my job. His wee chin wobbled as if he was about to cry too. I think he was ashamed of himself.

'But why didn't you tell me?' he kept saying over and over.

Then he apologised, taking his sweaty little palm and putting it in mine, and I didn't draw mine away. He told me the Inquiry changed their mind, don't want him today and are going to let him know when he'll be needed. It's cat and mouse stuff, like they're playing with him. I don't want him to go there again. It'll do for him.

He asked how Garry was about losing his Granny and I couldn't bring myself to explain, maybe I should have done then. I don't know but, with everything else, Garry, the 'little boy', seemed an irrelevance, mad. He'd wonder why I hadn't said anything before, wouldn't understand, what with the train and everything. He kept saying to me, almost chanting, that he was not 'going back' to the Inquiry ever, couldn't stand any more of it. I touched his brow and it was hot as an oven. I said, not to worry, I'd phone them etc., explain that he was too ill to return, but he insisted they'd never give up, keep trying to get him back, and even if, by some miracle, he survived that, he'd be put in jail like in France. I said, no, no, you'll be fine, it'll be over soon, no one puts ninety-year olds in prison etc. but nothing seemed to calm him. He raved on and on about it, exhausted himself, repeating himself. Surely, if they were going to put him in prison it would be here, in Scotland? I didn't know that could happen with these Inquiries. By his bed was one of those shitty poison pen letters, and that can't have helped anything.

Once he had quietened down, I began to tell him about Mum. I couldn't hold it back, just had to let it out. It's been days. How she'd been a librarian, but full of fun, a brave and beautiful woman and, in the middle of it, I found myself crying again, sobbing, and he squeezed my hand, trying to comfort me. I said she'd been a credit to the family, overcome difficulties, how if they'd met, if he'd known her, he'd have loved her, just like I did.

His eyes had closed. So, I decided I'd tell him everything, whether he was listening or could hear or not or even wanted to. I'd waited too long, missed her, but was not missing him. I began by saying about Mum being adopted, being born in Rosedean Hospital, Inverness, and, at that, I saw his eyelids flicker. I carried on with how I'd seen the papers at the Records Office, gave her Father's name and then her Grandfather's name. At that he tried to sit himself up but was too weak, so I got more pillows to prop him up. I brought out all the print-outs I'd got in my carrier bag and showed them to him, line by line. So, I said, at the end and hoping he would understand, 'You're my great Uncle.' He sighed and murmured: 'I knew it, felt it . . . always felt you were different.'

I told him I'd read the letter from him to my Gran, the one that had saved Mum, and me, I suppose. I said, thanks to him, we'd existed. He squeezed my hand again, saying, hoarsely; 'I can't tell you what this means to me and I . . .' His voice petered out into an extended cough. Seeing how cracked and dry his lips were, I went to the kitchen and got tea for him, lots of sugar, and some for me. As he was too shaky to lift the cup, I held it up to his lips while he took small sips. After about half an hour, he wriggled his hand along his bedclothes in order to take mine in his again and asked for me to get him pen and paper. I'm to drop off his letter this afternoon. I said I would but it's a fag, way out of my way, but he's got no chance otherwise.

If he's understood me, I think he believes me. I left him with his Family Book, smiling, whispering he'd always thought I'd a trace of Isabel about me, she was a looker too. I've taken his stripey pyjamas home with me, he'd wet them again. Seems funny, now he knows, me working for him, but, well, now I do it for the love, not just the money. Family. But I do need the money. I wonder if he's thought about that at all?

Doubt it, old men don't and I bet he's never worried about the rent.

Anyway, knowing that, at last, he knows about me, I feel like a different person. It's like the circle's complete, we've come in from the cold, become normal. I never felt a Whitadder anyway, for all I know about them, but I never felt related to Gran either and I wasn't any more than Mum was. Him and me, we're the family now

2nd June

Rough Andrea, as he calls her, had put his lunch tray by his bed where he couldn't reach it. One yoghurt, one tiny wee sandwich and one cup of cold soup. I tried to get him to eat something when I came, but he'd no appetite anymore and his breathing sounds like the hissing and chuff-chuff-chuff of an old-fashioned train. No breath to talk, just sucking air in tires him. 'Bee' chapped the door, so I took the flowers off her, but I said he was out. An eyebrow shot up. She'd only have exhausted him, he's not fit to see anybody, just sleeps most of the time. Looking daggers, she said she'd phone later as her mother was concerned about the Prof. 'Snap,' I replied, shutting the door. I wonder when he'll start telling people, introducing me as his Great Niece, or is he a snob, maybe not want to claim me? Bee with her dusty finger would faint. At about three o' clock, I could see Garry prowling about outside, so I flung open the window and told him to scoot in language he understands. I feel like the Prof's Staffie nowadays, snapping and snarling, protecting him from everyone.

When he woke, for a short while we looked at the book together. I liked the stuff about Elizabeth McCall in the late 1800s, who seems to have become Prince Louis of Battenburg's bidey.

'Your own great, great, great aunt, Miss Anstruther,' he whispered. I wanted to know more about her, but as we were talking about it (he's got a bracelet made of golden owls given her by the Prince!) the phone went again and, of course, it was Bee. I put the phone on speaker to help him hear her. She said her Mum had almost finished at the Inquiry, it had gone well except for some row about the date prison blood stopped being collected in the Inverness area (?), and then added that he was likely to be called back any day soon. I watched the colour literally drain from his face at those words and he began to tremble. Arsehole that she is, she made him cry.

3rd June

At yesterday's news he's gone into a decline. I did some dusting (in case Bee arrived again and somehow gained entry) and mopped the kitchen floor. I almost wished she would. Maybe I'd tell her my news, see her wince? He'd no proper work for me to do, so I just looked at some of his old papers in his study at random. For about an hour he sat in his chair in the sitting room, a bundle of documents by his slippers. I peeked a few times and he'd pick one up, glance at it, then put it down again. A few he dropped, but he didn't seem to care. Every so often he let out a sigh. To cheer him up, I went and got him a bunch of roses, but they could have been carrots for all the interest he took in them.

When I took him a cup of tea he was weeping again, tears running down his sharp little cheekbones and dripping off his chin. I'd like to have given him a cuddle but he's so tense I think he'd break in two. He kept repeating, once this is all over, you and I will be different, and, saying that, he pushed £400 in notes into my hand. Good. I need more zombies.

4th June

The call from the Inquiry came today. He took to his bed. He's to appear again on the 8th June. I said I can phone, like last time, put it off until you're better, but he just shook his head, unable to speak in his gloom.

I got him more lilies but he just turned his head away, waved me away.

I wake at about 4 a.m. every morning and remember there is no Mum.

5th June

I didn't manage to get to the phone in time and Eileen got to him. I could hear her huffing and puffing, stuttering, as it was still on speaker-phone. She was trying to ginger him up, telling him everything was 'f . . . f . . . fine' in her Dame Maggie accent, but I don't think she would have wasted her breath doing so if she'd seen him. He was yellow, holding the receiver away from himself as if it might bite his ear off. In his fright, he'd wet himself but I sorted it. I never thought I'd be able to touch these things, too squeamish by half, but because he's my Uncle, got nobody else, I can manage. She said he could get a doctor's certificate, keep them at bay, but I think he'd stopped listening by then as he was staring out of the window, seemed to have lost all focus. He didn't even say goodbye, just put the phone down.

6th June

When I arrived, I saw a letter on his bedside cabinet. It was addressed as usual to 'The Murderer'. Why the fuck didn't Andrea or Irma, whoever gave it to him, just toss it in the bin? I would have. He need never have known about it, instead he was a chittering wreck and that over and above this Court stuff coming up.

I took him a cup of tea, and looking me straight in the eyes, he asked me to kill him.

To kill him.

Right out, just like that. I was speechless, and that's a first.

He was gibbering a bit, but said it was fate, me coming into his life just when he needed me most. I was the One. Screamed at me that he couldn't face the Inquiry, couldn't think straight any more to protect himself, couldn't remember what happened yesterday, never mind thirty years ago and wasn't going to go to jail. His reputation would remain intact, he repeated, if he never went back, because Eileen had kept all her marbles and what she'd said would protect them all. When I said fine, don't go back, she'll look after you, he said, 'She can't keep me out of prison in France.' Whatever exactly that may mean.

'More letters, vile letters, more and more letters,' he said.

Then he added, in a hoarse, weak little voice, 'And I'm losing mine, my mind's not the same'. I shook my head, trying to pretend it was all a joke or nonsense or something, but he wouldn't stop, kept saying it over and over. Wailed that he mustn't let his family down, all those people, he was the last of the line and it couldn't end with a jailbird. Every one of them had done something to make him proud, he wasn't being the one to let them all down.

Joking, I said, you've forgotten someone, haven't you? I'm the last of the line now! He slurred something about little Garry and then said, holding my eye and sounding quite sane: 'Please, Jean. Once, I saved you, your mother. Now you can save me.' I said no chance, he must be kidding, then I'd go to prison, but he promised, sounded even sensible, that when ninety-year-olds die, it's always considered natural causes, old age. No one bothers to do a Post Mortem, apparently, when they die at home like he would. Why would they, I suppose? No one lives forever, so no risk either. 'Exactly, no risk, no risk,' he kept repeating. 'I wouldn't ask if I thought there was – you and Garry are too important to me. I'm dying anyway.' He's the doctor, must know about these things. All I'd have to do was push a pillow on his face, he said, and he'd hardly resist, but then he'd be free, have let no one down, and I would have returned the favour he once did me. No one else would do it. I had to be The One.

I didn't know what to do. Looked hard at him, yellow, breathless, made of paper, frightened witless. If he'd been a dog, an old cat, I'd not have hesitated for a second.

So, what the fuck else could I do? I'd seen how terrified, how terrorised, old, incontinent and decrepit he was, how unhappy, muddled, and disabled he was. At first hand, close up to my face, day after sodding day. He wanted to die, and, to be honest, who could blame him? There was no pill to put him right. Time would not heal him, only make everything worse and worse again. I knew him well enough to know what mattered to him, how his ancestors comforted him, how he would suffer at the thought of his own disgrace. I should do. He is my blood, now my responsibility and only mine. He and Mum will meet at last.

Nobody else would do it.

So, in that instant I broke, I did it. I put a pillow over his face and pressed hard. And he was as good as his word, hardly struggled at all, seemed no more than a little bird fluttering about. I suppose it took seconds but it felt like forever. I did it and I can't take it back, change my mind, right thing to do, right thing to do. God help me.

Before I left, I kissed his little baldy scalp. I am the last of the line now.

7th June

A tall polis woman came to my house today. I was in bed, brain bathed in rum, but jumped out, kept my nerve, pretended to be surprised on hearing of the Prof's death. Collapsing onto the settee in shock, bum pinning down my shaking hands, I explained that I'd left him last night in bed, alive and well, though exhausted. I didn't know Andrea or Irma's address but I told her about them, might muddy the waters a bit. Not to mention the mad letter-writers with their name-calling. She stared hard at me, asked if I was alright. Christ! So much for dying of sodding old age! Prof, what have you done to me? This was not supposed to happen. I trusted you. No polis were supposed to be involved.

Looking up at her, I nearly shat myself with fright but, somehow, I managed to stay calm. How am I going to survive now? I've no money (again) and no job (again). If he's left me something (everything?), I'll have to wait an age. Garry was useful for the rent too. If the Prof's right, this will all pass, everything will be just fine. This will just be a formality, done in every case. He promised me.

Shut up. Shut up. Shut up.

8th June

They came and questioned me again. I stuck to my story, but I said how ancient he was, fragile as wet tissue. Wanted to go. He died in bed, for heaven's sake, just what you'd pray for, what anyone would want. Doesn't anyone die of old age anymore? What am I going to do? I went for a drink with Lena to get the zombies (a blue buzz cut does nothing for anybody), but all she can talk about is Simon (42), her new boss. Availability seems to be his sole virtue. I said 'Watch out, at that age availability may not be a recommendation.'

'What d'you mean?'

'Bet he lives with his Mum?'

That shut her up.

Thanks to the dope, she wasn't really there anyway. I hoped a couple more vodkas might calm me down but they just made me jittery, jumpy, my hands alive and doing their own thing. I keep reminding myself of what the Prof said, he wouldn't have asked me to help if I'd be likely to be caught. I believe that, have to keep reminding myself of that. Now I really know how he felt, the thought of prison terrifies me, fills my mind endlessly.

The giant polis lady kept asking me about his pyjamas. I told them I took his stuff home, wasn't even paid for the work I'd done. She looked down on me, in every way possible.

11th June

Hallelujah! No polis, no nothing for two days, three if you count today. Maybe they've decided he did die of old age. After a top-up of rum, I went for a job interview at Mario's Restaurant, just dishwashing, but it'd tide me over. The tricksy Italian Mamma interviewing me asked if I knew how to operate a Transkell 6 Dish Washing Machine and, naturally, I said yes. I could learn. After all, how difficult could it be? So, bustling ahead of me and releasing a slip-stream of BO as she strode onwards, she took me to it. Or, at least, I thought she did. Then she watched as I tried to load dishes into a commercial oven. She pursed her lips tight, gestured for the return of the overall and escorted me to the door. I am determined to better myself. Having money will help. Every night I think of the Prof, dream about him, Mum and about IT. How did I manage? Why the hell did I do it for him? I did the right thing but, God, I wish I hadn't. But I didn't let him down, didn't let Mum down either.

I did what they asked.

Garry came and made a nuisance of himself at my front door. I let him in and I was so low after the interview, scared too, that I let him paw me. Am I mad? He asked why I had lost my job, etc. etc., so I said the old man had died and he said, 'He'll be burning up in the flames now with all the other shoplifters.' I am mad.

14th June

When I came back from an interview I missed by going to the wrong place, two polis men were at home and took me, and a bag, to the station at Portobello. Some unshaven bloke in a shiny suit in there told me he was the 'Duty Solicitor' and would look after me. I'm to be charged. He smelt of chips, and the buttons of his white shirt over his belly were coming loose. His vest was a Hibs T-shirt. I couldn't think, couldn't hear, couldn't breathe. My mind had fled. Like he said, I answered 'No comment' to everything the superintendent asked. At the end I was given a bit of paper, saying that I was charged with MURDERING the Prof. Fuck, fuck, fuck. I wish I had never taken his job, found out who I am, listened to his weasel words. He's alright, safe, right out of it, but he's dropped me in it, good and proper, in his place. What came over me, listening to him? Maybe he didn't even care, thought about himself alone. I'm to spend the night here and go to Court tomorrow. Thank God, Mum is dead, I nearly said this will kill her. I forgot my pajamas and will have to sleep in my bra and pants. With all those threatening letters from the poison pen freaks, you'd think they'd have pounced on them, not me. They threatened him, told him they were going to kill him. Good as did it and made his life hell.

15th June

Jan, the security person, hustled me into an old, fusty wood-panelled courtroom. Said I looked pale, was I alright? No, but no one cares. In there, the lawyers mumble this and mumble that to each other and I just let Stan, my solicitor, do it all. He answers for me and they all seem to know what they are talking about. I feel numb, as if it's happening to somebody else. While they were gabbing with each other, a pigeon crashed into the main window and I watched it slide down the pane, thick blood oozing and a few grey feathers drifting away. One of the security men winked at me but I didn't wink back. Despite Stan the Man's mutterings for me, there's to be no bail for the wicked. Saughton is my destination, on remand. Why not Cornton Vale? It's for women surely? Katy, the Sergeant, said I'd get on fine and that the security staff in Saughton were nice people. Her first cousin (Sue) works, as a civilian, in the library. Sue told her it was quite a change from the Corstorphine Public Library, her main assistant is a paedophile and she spends her time helping them out on Clink Radio. Julian Clary has been on, apparently.

I cannot fight this, do not know who to trust. I'm on my own.

10th August 2014

Another lawyer QC came to see me today together with Stan. Stan's got a new shirt, stripey, one that he can button up but I could still see the Hibs green through it. I told the QC that I had not done it, was not guilty, and had left the Prof hale and hearty as I'd found him. I said that it must have been old age, natural causes and someone, somewhere was making a big mistake. I'm not admitting to murder! Christ, I'd never get out, people would think I'm like that blonde Hindley woman.

I can't spend the rest of my life here.

The QC said OK, they would contact some kind of forensic expert on my behalf and that 'homicidal' asphyxiation was notoriously difficult to prove and 'of course, the onus (?) is on the Crown'. 'They have to prove you did it, you don't have to prove you didn't', Stan said, translating for me. 'Goody,' I replied. The QC could, he added, looking at me beadily, only put forward a not guilty plea if I really hadn't done it. I nodded. 'They have to prove you did it, you don't have to prove you didn't,' he repeated, as if I'm a moron. 'Also, the evidence against you is all circumstantial.'

'And?' I said.

'No one saw you do it. They'll also have to prove you, as opposed to anyone else, did it.'

'They have no evidence I did it because I didn't,' I said. I didn't murder him, I saved him.

The QC's a big man, big-bellied and big-boned but I'd put money on it that his grey curls are made of nylon. Odd, he must earn a packet and could, presumably, get real hair from somewhere, China perhaps? They're all black-haired after all, and must go grey. In all of Edinburgh, I've never seen a bald Chinaman. They told me that the Crown have got CCTV of me coming and going, but that proves nothing, I'm not denying that I was there, am I? I told them I'd been. Stan muttered something about the prosecution case, money coming to me from the Prof under his will, but I said I'd no idea of anything like that. I bloody don't either, although it should, God knows, I'm his blood. The QC said, 'Of course, if she's found guilty of murder that'll be forfeited' or something like that. When I get out, when all of this has gone away, I am going to let out my secret to the WHOLE BLOODY WORLD but I can't now. Only when I'm cleared can I be an Anstruther, then I'm going to make something of my life, of me. Maybe go to University, I could do better than Stan, I know that much. I am going to change my name. I'll keep Jean but be JEAN MARY ANSTRUTHER. Maybe, one day I will have a child and show it the Family Book. The first thing that I'm going to do once I get out of here is get that book back and do the entries for the Prof and my Gran. A warder person googled her for me on her phone and stuff came up, so there's plenty to write about. She exhibited in London Galleries, won a scholarship and taught at Glasgow School of Art. She amounted to someone too, never married and died in a road traffic accident when she was 38. I wish Mum could have known her, I wish I could have known her. I wish she was here with me now. Maybe she is, maybe they all are.

21st August

Another day when I have sat all day in the dock and feel sick to my stomach. That bitch, Andrea, was on and lost no opportunity to put the boot in, saying I didn't do my work properly, took things and pulled the wool, generally, over the Prof's eyes. I must remind Stan or my QC that he gave me that silver stuff and the bracelet, like I told the police. The only thing I took, and they needn't know this, was the Family Book, and I can't explain that now. The prosecutor's forensic Doc person sounded mighty convincing I thought, and I saw someone on the Jury nodding at everything he said, another was taking down notes and two women looked as if they could not take their eyes off him, would like to eat him up. The prosecuting lady seems reliable as a robot, speaks like Siri, never errs or umms and radiates control. She behaves like a winner.

When my QC tried to shake what the Doc said (murder by smothering) I reckon he got nowhere, the Doc just repeated everything slowly as if for a six-year-old and sounded even more convincing. Why would you get him to do that? Not surprisingly, perhaps, the Jury were gobbling it up. Stan, winking, told me not to look so worried, my expert is 'the Biz', has something up her sleeve and will blow Beamish out of the water.

22nd August 2014

The shit has hit the fan. Whilst my so-called expert forensic woman, Dr Willow (looking as if she had just left primary school) was being questioned by the Robot, I noted that the Lady Judge was wrinkling her nose, shaking her head and catching the eye of the Robot.

Willow was saying something like the only real evidence for smothering, as opposed to a natural death, was the bruising and abrasions on the inside of the lips. Then she said, looking like a cat with cream dripping off its whiskers, that those findings were easily explained away.

'How?' asked the clever Robot.

'By the resuscitation procedures, it's all caused by the mouth to mouth and the CPR etc. Everything can be explained by that . . . the damage was done by the paramedics, it doesn't suggest compression of the nose and mouth by the accused.'

She said something like that anyway.

The Robot pauses and then asks Tit Willow if she's read the Post Mortem report and the Tit nods her head.

'Well then,' the Robot begins 'you must have seen that there were no resuscitation procedures used on Professor Anstruther? Look at para one of Dr Beamish's report, please.'

'Eh? None at all?' Tit Willow cheeps, five octaves up, her head down looking at the document.

'None at all.' the Robot confirms. 'So, in the absence of that explanation, would you agree with me that the most likely explanation, indeed only explanation, for the bruising and abrasions is smothering?'

NO, NO, NO, I glare from the dock.

' Er . . . er . . . yes,' Tit Willow says, throwing a panic-stricken glance at my QC.

Meanwhile, the Jury appeared very uncomfortable, bemused, unwilling to look me in the face.

I heard my QC say 'Shit!' under his breath.

Then he hissed 'Shit, and double shit!' towards Stan, looking daggers at him, before whispering quite loudly, 'Is this her first? Where exactly did you find her? At a Job Centre?'

Did he want the Judge to hear?

Stan hissed, 'I told you, Dr Kurashi was not available.'

Meanwhile, the Jury were fidgeting, bottom-shuffling in their seats and looking everywhere except at me. I'd had enough. So, I gestured to Stan and told him I needed, urgently, to speak to him and my QC. In the teeth of opposition, Crabbie persuaded the Judge we should have a break. I asked Crabbie outright if we were doomed and, looking at Stan as if he was a dogshit, he said through gritted teeth, 'Things are not going as well as I expected, certainly.'

'That's a yes, is it?'

Crabbie nodded.

'Right,' I said, 'I'm going to tell you the truth, the real truth and nothing but the truth.' So, I told them that I'd done it, then I explained why. Said I had to, I was the Prof's only relative, he begged me, I told them they could look at Mum's adoption record stuff, see she was the daughter of Isabel Anstruther. See Isabel's birth certificate. See my birth certificate, showing I was Mum's daughter.

'But why didn't you tell us this in the first place?' the QC says crossly.

'And plead guilty? I didn't murder him, they were saying I'd murdered him. I didn't know how to explain . . . that I'd done it but I also hadn't done it.'

'Convenient all this stuff too,' Stan says in a nasty, sly way. 'Remarkable coincidence . . . truly remarkable.'

'Convenient for me? No. For the Prof? Certainly,' I said, furious with the fat turd. 'If it hadn't been for him, begging me, begging me to save him, like I said, I'd not have killed him. No one else would have helped him, saved him . . . he had no one else. I was his only family, the only one that would take the risk for him . . . a bloody unlucky coincidence for me.'

'Mmm,' says Stan, looking at Crabbie.

'Well, let's see what we've got, what you've got to

show us. Nothing much to lose now!' the QC says, as if humouring me.

I got my phone sent from Saughton and showed them the photos I had of Mum's birth certificate, the digest and Isabel's certificate too. Everything I have, all the stuff. I told them the story, that she was dead and I was his only living relative. Told them about the Prof's anti-abortion letter, saving Mum, saving me. I described how I had watched him go downhill over the months I was with him, watched him sweat blood over the Inquiry, fear he was going to be put in prison in France and that he had begged me, begged me, to release him. Told them Mum had died. Thinking about it, I began to cry. 'What about the money?' Stan said. 'The Crown think you killed him for that, knowing about the will.' I said that I had delivered the letter but I knew nothing of what it said but, actually, it reinforced what I was saying. The Prof was, above all other things, concerned about his line, his bloodline, family, ancestors and those sorts of things. He would only have changed it, left me any money because he was glad he had family. I was his family.

'It didn't say, the will, I mean, that you were his long-lost great niece?'

'I never saw it, I don't know what it said. BUT I did see him when I gave him the pen. He could hardly lift a spoon, it's a miracle he could write at all . . . he . . .'

'For pity's sake, Miss Whitadder, why didn't you tell me the truth, all of this before?' Crabbie butted in, eyes narrowed. 'How can anyone trust you now? How can I trust you, go on representing you?'

'I've already told you. Because . . . I was charged with MURDER, I was scared shitless. Mum died. He, the Prof, promised me this would not happen, and it has. I had done it, I did kill him, but only because he begged me to save him. I had to. He was desperate to go, couldn't do it himself. If I said I'd done it, well, it would all be over for me and I'd be in prison forever, for my life. Wouldn't I? You told me smothering was difficult to prove, the circumstantial bit too, I'd a chance again to get off completely. Because I didn't want to admit such a terrible thing, because admitting I killed my own relative . . . worse, far worse than a stranger. I am not a murderer.'

'It's a right mess,' Stan said.

The QC shook his head, then they looked each other in the eye and said together: 'A Culpable Homicide plea?'

'Balance of mind gone? An act of love, of mercy?' The QC clapped his hands together.

'Why would they go for that?' I asked, baffled by everything including their jargon. 'They're winning . . .'

'Because,' Stan says, 'the prosecution, to "win" as you put it, must prove two things: that the victim was smothered AND that you did it. The second bit's difficult too, they know that. So, they'll probably be happy with a Guilty plea to Culpable Homicide. Someone has been smothered and there could still be a Not Guilty verdict. Prosecutors don't like that. If we can just get a supportive psych report?'

'What's a psych report?' I asked.

The QC nodded, 'A report from a psychiatrist to confirm your state of mind when you did the deed. It's worth a punt?'

'What do you mean?' I asked.

'It's technical,' Crabbie said. 'You loved the Prof?'

'Yes.'

'You witnessed his unbearable suffering . . . it affected you, depressed you? Perhaps, you lost your mind, caused the death but only because the Prof asked you to do so, your guilt is less than in the case of murder. If so, Culpable Homicide fits the bill . . .'

That's the gist. It's what we all meant, I think, and roughly how it was said. I couldn't write it down then and there, but I think it's right enough.

After a phone call, I may be going to see a shrink next week, apparently. What a fuck up. Now, I've (even if I survive) brought shame upon me and them, the Anstruthers, but not as much as if I was a murderer. Why the hell did the lawyers assure me I'd get off? Fool, to believe them, to believe him, to believe anybody.

With much harrumphing, 'No guarantees' (I wouldn't believe them if they did give them), they left me 'to go and talk to the other side'. About three hours later they came back, Crabbie grinning and his wig halfway down his forehead and said, 'Praise the Lord, they're considering it!'

I said, 'What happens next?'

So, I am going back to that hellhole, am to see this

psychiatrist next week, apparently. Then a decision may be made.

'If it succeeds?' I asked, 'what then?'

Stan, as if telling me I've won the lottery says: 'You'll be sentenced but, if they accept the plea and with luck, you'll only get a couple of years, three at most.'

Lucky me.

NOTE FOR MR SPARROW

This time they were right. Four visits from the shrink and three years exactly, though I may get out before with 'Good Behaviour'. The Solicitor, Mr Menzies, came to call one day. He told me about the Prof's (I can't get used to calling him anything else) will. He explained that with a Murder conviction I'd have forfeited the money, have no chance, but that I did have an outside chance of getting something with my Culpable Homicide conviction. I'll not hold my breath. He'll sell up the house and stuff and set things in motion for the charities and me in that respect.

In the meanwhile, I while away my days learning new things. I attend Italian classes, Sophia who's in for pimping, is helping me there; cookery, too, and I began yesterday a new module in my Open University Law Course. Garry's been to visit me a few times, brought me a nice jersey. Oh, and the paedophile is no longer the number one library assistant, I am, old hand that I've become.

I'll make something of my life, prove myself worthy of

the Prof, my real Gran, my mum and all the others in our family. I know what I did and why I did it. I'm not guilty, and I haven't let them down.

[press cutting]
The Times (24th August 2014)

MURDER TRIAL
UNEXPECTEDLY ADJOURNED

The trial of a former care worker, Ms Jean Whitadder, was halted two days ago in dramatic circumstances. Prosecution evidence had been led to prove that the 30-year-old woman had smothered her elderly employer, Professor Sir Alexander Anstruther, with his own pillow. Forensic evidence provided in her defence by an expert pathologist, Dr Clara Willow, was successfully challenged at a relatively early stage by the prosecution. To the clear surprise of all present in the Court, under pressure, Dr Willow conceded that she had made a mistake and that the evidence did suggest that the Professor had, indeed, been suffocated. At that juncture, the Defence Counsel, George Crabbie QC, sought a brief adjournment from the trial Judge and was granted it.

CARE WORKER KILLED HER
OWN GREAT UNCLE

In very unusual circumstances, a former Care Worker, Ms Jean Whitadder, was yesterday given a three-year sentence for the culpable homicide of Professor Sir Alexander Anstruther.

Professor Anstruther was found dead in his home in Duddingston Village, Edinburgh, having been smothered with his own pillow by the convicted woman. Her plea of guilty to the lesser charge due to diminished responsibility was accepted by the Crown following less than one week of evidence at her trial for murder at the High Court in Edinburgh.

The Presiding Judge, Lady Johnson, said Whitadder's was 'a tragic and truly exceptional case'. Professor Anstruther had once been an eminent physician, but by the time he encountered Jean Whitadder he had long since retired from all professional activities and was a frail, confused 90-year-old. He was lonely and, as a result of his participation in the ongoing Goodhart Inquiry, under unbearable stress. Ms Whitadder, whose mother was adopted, befriended him and became very fond of her elderly employer as he did of her. Through a series of unexpected events, resulting in genealogical research, she discovered that she was, in fact, her employer's great niece, and only remaining family. The Professor, suffering from Alzheimer's Disease, had become convinced that he would be discredited by the Inquiry and be sent to prison.

Following the recent death of her own mother and having witnessed the Professor's daily suffering at close quarters and over many months, when he had begged her to 'put him out of his misery' she had, finally, acceded to his request and smothered him with his own pillow. A psychiatrist provided a report suggesting that Ms Whitadder had been subjected to unimaginable stress as a result of her mother's death and her daily exposure to her beloved great uncle's tragic decline. She also had a personality disorder making her more vulnerable to psychotic episodes such as she had been subject to at the time of the offence. George Crabbie Q.C., in mitigation, said Ms Whitadder now found her own action 'quite dreadful, as she had recovered some insight'. Lady Johnson noted that in the well-nigh unique circumstances of the case only a very light sentence would be appropriate. Hearing the Judge's words, Ms Whitadder broke down in tears and was led out of the Court to begin her sentence.

DOCUMENT C

PSYCHIATRIC REPORT ON
MS JEAN MARY WHITADDER
(DOB 24/6/1984)
BY DR ANDREW HAROLD
PEEL CLINIC
ST BERNARD'S TERRACE
EDINBURGH

23rd September 2014

INTRODUCTION

This report was commissioned by Hogg Defence Lawyers
with the purpose of assisting the Court in its considera-
tion of the extent of the legal responsibility that Jean Mary
Whitadder may have for the act that led to the death of
Professor Sir Alexander Anstruther in his house on 6/7
June 2014.

I am a consultant psychiatrist with a specialist training
in forensic psychiatry. I hold a consultant position as
part of the medical team at the Peel Clinic, St Bernard's
Terrace, Edinburgh, and an honorary senior lecturer post
at the University of Edinburgh Centre for Clinical Brain
Science. In order to prepare this report, I interviewed the
accused at HMP Saughton on four occasions. I also discussed her clinical condition with the visiting psychiatrist

then responsible for her care. He confirmed my impression that she was recovering from a severe depressive episode with psychotic features. She was then on a high dose of antidepressants and lithium treatment instituted following a self-harming attempt made after trial was adjourned. Her clinical state required the interviews to be short – hence their number – and she was co-operative throughout. Her recollection of the relevant period is muddled, undoubtedly in consequence of the effects of her current drug regime. As a result, I had to question her very carefully in order to draw out from her, in so far as possible, a coherent account of the events over that period.

SUMMARY OF OPINION

In Jean Whitadder's case there are two diagnosable psychiatric conditions present. Firstly, a personality disorder, present since late adolescence and of moderate severity. Secondly, Bipolar Disorder Type 1, in that she is currently recovering from a severe depressive episode with psychotic features. In all probability, she played her part in the death of Sir Alexander Anstruther while in a manic, or mixed affective, state with psychotic features. These psychotic manic and depressive episodes are the first in her life, although she has suffered minor depressive episodes, or periods of prolonged dysphoria throughout her early adult years. As to whether a mental disorder of a type or severity to impair her legal responsibility for her actions was present at the time, I can confirm that this is so, and that, in my opinion, this is not a borderline case.

PERSONAL DEVELOPMENT

Ms Jean Whitadder's birth was normal. She is the only child of Susan and Ian Whitadder. Contact, since early childhood, with her father has been minimal. Susan Whitadder returned to her work in the Dunbar Library soon after giving birth. She had been adopted as an infant, following her birth to Isabel Anstruther, the now deceased sister of Professor Sir Alexander Anstruther. Susan was aware that she had been adopted but not of the identity of her biological parents

Jean Whitadder's recollections suggest a relatively fraught and materially deprived early childhood. Her grandmother occasionally helped out with childcare but her grandfather died when she was only 7 years old. Following a period of ill-health, the grandmother too died in Jean's late adolescence. Whilst she was ill, the mother and daughter relationship – which throughout early and late childhood had been an exceptionally close and confiding one – altered in a number of respects. Secrets began to be kept; there was anger and mistrustfulness on both sides, culminating in a period of estrangement and Jean leaving the family home to live in her own flat. The grandmother's ill-health (a state of affairs which preoccupied Susan Whitadder), coincided with the first appearances of a pattern of emotional reactivity and risky behavior in Jean which went on to characterise a number of her personal and interpersonal priorities during her twenties. Jean considers that her grandmother's illness and her mother's preoccupation with it was the cause of this pattern. I take a different view. It is much more likely that what is being described is the development of an abnormality of personality, an understanding of which can both explain the unusual mixture of recurring difficulties she faced throughout early adulthood, and her vulnerability to the brief but severe mental disorder she suffered from on 6 June 2014.

During the period of estrangement Jean lived on her own, required to be self-reliant. She disliked both these things. In her mid-teens, she had started to under-perform at school and was a group truant for the last two years. During this period, she had her first prolonged period of dysphoria, largely unremarked upon by the school, and unnoticed by Susan because of her preoccupation with her own mother's increasing ill-health. Jean discovered that starving herself for a few days took much of the edge off the mood, and the depression could be kept at bay by such a regime every fortnight or so. Eventually this effort at relief failed, and other techniques were explored – binge drinking, cannabis, casual sexual encounters – with varying but unpredictable success. This pattern of attempting to control a depressed mood by various self-injuring behaviors became more central to her life around her grandmother's final illness and death, and her awareness of the short-term utility, but long-term futility, of this kind of self-control led to her first panic attack a few days after her grandmother's funeral.

An important motivation to acquiring her own flat was the belief (subsequently found to be false) that she was pregnant, father unclear. This belief gave rise to her first encounter with ambivalence, which she recollects as a period of utter confusion. Initially she was pleased, experiencing an enhanced sense of connection with her mother through the circle of life and other similarities, including the prospect of child-rearing without a partner. Then her attitude changed and her pregnancy became suddenly very unwelcome to her: she excoriated herself for the fecklessness of the conception, her own unsuitability for care giving; she came to see herself as the ruin of her mother's life by forcing her into wedlock to an unreliable husband and resolved to terminate the pregnancy. On the natural resumption of her menstrual cycle, Jean had her first episode of depersonalisation, a troubling and pervasive perception that the world, and the people in it, are not real, but imitations of themselves, seemingly made of cardboard, or acting as puppets, or robots. Although she had not undergone a termination, she knew she had intended to 'kill the baby' as she put it. Having known at school some troubled classmates who cut themselves, she tried it and got some relief from it briefly, as did frightening herself – standing on high ledges, running heedless into traffic – so, as with the depressed mood at school and starving herself, she explored various ways of reducing the sense of alienation from the depersonalisation feelings in the months after her intended termination. What ended this was the longed-for rapprochement with her mother.

Following the rapprochement, Jean became employed at the Blackhall library alongside her mother. These eighteen months are the longest continuous period of work that Jean has had. During them, she acquired familiarity and competence with the database systems library groups use in collection-building and so forth, a skill later useful in her employment by Sir Alexander Anstruther. Skill-based employment had not been a feature of Jean's work history: her preference was for unskilled work – call-centres, reception desks, hotels – and she comments insightfully about this. Skilled work usually involves working as part of a team, which means working relationships which, for her, start well but rapidly deteriorate – tension, criticism, hostility – whereas, casual unskilled work carries few expectations of that sort. 'People, apart from my Mum,' she said, 'never get me.'

By her mid-twenties, there was little to show of the promise that Jean's early teenage years presaged. She was markedly underqualified for the type of job which her general intelligence suggested she might be capable of. She had a restricted social life, with a succession of desultory and short-lived sexual relationships; and most of her school friendships disintegrated as her friends, unlike her, moved on to the family life stage. In addition, she was often experiencing difficulties with her state of mind: panic attacks, depressed mood and depersonalisation were present alone or in combination. Regimes of food restriction, risky behaviour, avoidance of emotional intimacy, inhibition of personal ambition had become the established pattern. Despair and depression at their worst made work sometimes difficult. Her beloved mother, who throughout Jean's twenties remained a constant reassuring presence, encouraged her to seek help, but for both of them, this was a fraught subject. Jean was very clear that she did not deserve help: how her life was, and is, is the result of a series of personal failings and poor decisions for which she holds herself entirely responsible. She declined help, such as counselling, worrying that it would amount to little more than intrusive criticism and might make her more vividly aware of her shortcomings; what she wanted was a transformative opportunity, to become 'a Success'. How, she did not address.

In 2012 there was a sustained reduction in the overall severity of Jean's mood and neurotic symptoms, following her starting a relationship with Garry Hudson (36). This is the longest lasting sexual relationship Jean has had. The basis of its success was his willingness to accommodate, firstly, the degree of emotional distance she required between them, and, secondly, her continued closeness and dependence on her mother.

However, it was during this relationship that the next domain of psychological disturbance became manifest. Pre their cohabitation, Jean occasionally felt that she was being followed as she walked home from Garry's flat to her own; hearing footsteps or glimpsing someone in shadows. Often it would just be a prickling sensation in her scalp and neck which she attributed to a subconscious awareness of a nearby menacing presence. At first, she thought that it might be Garry playing a joke, to spook her into staying longer with him, but then thought that it might be someone from her past, jealous of this new relationship and seeking to spoil it. Garry denied following her. She vacillated between being concerned about who might be following her and about how intrusive and dominating this paranoid feeling was. She also worried whether she could support herself with this extra burden of mental trouble. Shortly after the appearance of this symptom, she started noticing small signs that someone had been in her flat – objects moved; slight, unfamiliar smells – and began to fear for her sanity. Unfortunately, at about the time she decided to tell her mother about this fear, her mother's illness became apparent. In January 2014 Stage IV carcinoma of the lung was diagnosed, with a six-month survival prognosis. In consequence of her mother's illness Jean was unable to confide in her or get the usual psychological support that she provided. Consequently, Jean returned to her cutting behaviour and reintroduced her periodic bouts of self-starvation.

Jean said that at all times throughout her much loved mother's illness and suffering she was acutely aware of her own inability to help, her own complete powerlessness.

In the weeks shortly after the diagnosis, Jean had responded to a job advertisement in the local newspaper (found by her mother).

SUMMARY

The extent of personal and behavioural disturbance outlined above is sufficient to support a diagnosis of Personality Disorder ICD-10 revision, F60.9.

The importance of the diagnosis of Personality NOS (Not Otherwise Specified) to the present situation is that it identifies a vulnerability to a wide variety of psychiatric disorder episodes, both psychotic and non-psychotic. It also plays an explanatory role when we come to consider the abnormal degree of social isolation in which the events and actions described below took place. The Disorder also determines certain of the features of the attachments Jean has: intense, exclusive, unstable, protective. It also accounts for the small number of other relationships she has had which do not contain such features. The same features tend to recur in her relationships; an idealisation of the person, a dread of their leaving or coming to harm and emotional turbulence in the day to day conduct of that relationship. It could therefore be anticipated in Jean's case that her response to her mother's death would be to become over-protective and harm-preventing in any other relationships, particularly that with Sir Alexander, whom she would perceive as being reliant on her, in need of her protection.

EMPLOYMENT AT DUDDINGSTON MANSE

Jean was employed, in short, to organise her employer's chaotic paperwork, particularly that relevant to the impending Inquiry. This work resulted in a deep, protective fondness for her employer (an unusual experience for her) and her fondness was reciprocated. She began to believe that powerful forces were ranged against her frail, elderly employer. They consisted of those in the establishment responsible for ensuring that no inquiry had taken place, despite the passage of almost four decades since the contaminated blood scandal occurred. She became convinced that they would not want her employer to assist the Inquiry.

Through familial research and Jean's perusal of her employer's papers, she became aware of their blood tie (Sir Alexander is her great uncle) and, crucially, of the fact that but for her employer's actions, neither she nor her mother would have existed.

Jean's awareness of her employer's fragility, both physical and mental, was increased when he was accused of shoplifting at a local supermarket. She witnessed its effect upon him, including his rapid mental decline thereafter. Her perception of her own role as his protector strengthened as a result of that episode and its aftermath.

Jean came to believe that the powerful establishment forces were determined to ensure that her employer could not give his evidence and implicate them. She realised that, unprepared for the Inquiry, unable to answer questions, he would have posed no threat to them. Ironically, in assisting him with the organisation of his papers, she had increased the danger to him arising from his appearance at it. Consequently, she felt guilty and became frantic and watchful on his behalf.

Jean also saw abusive, threatening letters sent to her employer's from former patients' families or victim groups and witnessed their effect on her employer. She was subject to significant emotional pressure outside of work, witnessing, powerlessly, her mother's suffering and decline. She considered the staff unhelpful to her mother and unsympathetic to her. Jean felt hostile and resentful towards the staff, seeing them as another powerful establishment force, once more exerting a malign influence.

She came to believe that Garry had been conscripted by such malevolent, powerful forces. She interpreted his arresting of her employer as a means devised by them of damaging her employer, reducing his ability to withstand the rigours of the Inquiry. She confronted him with her beliefs. This ended their relationship and, in turn, adversely affected the quantity and quality of Jean's sleep.

She began to see similarities between the hostile hospital powers and those powers hostile to her employer. Powerless against the former, she was determined not to assist in any way those who wished to damage Sir Alexander. Having seen the effect on her mother's mind of medication, she became concerned that her employer's mind should not be damaged by drugs or poisons. To this end, she scrutinised and disposed of many foodstuffs in the Duddingston Manse, satisfying herself by this means that he would remain safe.

Whilst Sir Alexander was giving his evidence, Susan Whitadder died. Jean was present when she died and witnessed the excruciating pain she endured shortly before her end. Alone, she attended to all the many requirements following thereon, including the arrangements for the funeral. Her recollection of her state of mind during the immediate bereavement period was of complete emptiness, behaving like an automaton, only being able to think about matters which made her fearful, obsessing about how to protect her employer from harm. The quality and quantity of her sleep further declined.

When Jean returned to the Anstruther house at the end of May, exhausted, she noticed a considerable decline in her employer's physical state and his mental acuity.

She concluded that in her absence, the malevolent forces that she feared had somehow got to him, disabled him. She searched the premises for signs of poisoned food or drink. Sometimes, she herself considered such thinking 'Mad' but, at other times, found herself completely swayed by it and in awe of the powers that had been able to achieve such a result.

In this time of extreme confusion, she heard her mother say: 'It's easier to leave if something is left behind.'

She felt her mother's presence strongly and did not doubt who had said it. Her own response ('What do you mean, Mum?') seemed alien, robotic and ethereal to her. At this point, she still did not understand what her mother meant. Did it mean Susan Whitadder had found her own death easier to face in the knowledge that she, Jean, was left behind? Or did it mean that Sir Alexander, Susan's uncle, could now let go of his life as the family line continued on through her, Jean?

Then her mother said, 'You could not help me, but you can help him.'

'Him,' she somehow knew, was Sir Alexander, although she did not then understand what 'help' her mother was referring to. This was an epiphany for Jean: she now felt that the living and the dead were penetrating her mind, knew her and her thoughts. At this point, she could trust nothing that came into her awareness: thoughts could come from her, or from the dead, or others living.

On 6 June 2014 Sir Alexander introduced the topic of his own death, and how he longed for it, for peace. He used the trigger word 'help'. She had witnessed his decline, believed him when he said he had something terminal, was dying already. She took his assurance, that at his age there would be no post mortem, as gospel due to his eminent medical standing. Equally, she understood his plea to her that she should be the one to 'Save' him now just as he had once saved her as a result of his entreaties to his sister not to have an abortion. He, unlike her, had not been prepared to 'Kill the baby', she repeated several times.

Her thinking about his proposal came to be dominated by associations that lent the enterprise a terrifying grandeur, as she felt increasingly in contact – in some sense – with both the living and the dead. Her feeling of uniqueness at this point was underscored by her realisation that she would be the one to let (a) her mother finally meet the relative who made her life possible, and (b) let him finally be reunited with the rest of his family. She was filled with dread and excitement, conscious of her own important place in his life and, potentially, the blessed release that would be his death. She saw herself as The Chosen One.

Simultaneously, Jean recoiled from his suggestion due to her horror of the act and her love for the old man. She did not want to lose him. In addition, she retained a degree of fear about her imprisonment should she be caught. Ultimately, she convinced herself that if her love meant anything, she must put his wishes above her own and reunite him with those he now wished to be with and ensure that he, unlike her mother, did not suffer a painful death. Her sacrifice would be her 'Success'.

DIAGNOSTIC FORMULATION

It is important to bear in mind that the period in which this psychosis arose was one of profound affective disturbance, where the normal features – self-neglect and self-absorption, pessimism, loss of energy, guilt, anger – are present but in a somewhat altered form, so that they can be difficult to spot when the abnormal mood and thinking arrive. They also modify the abnormal mood and thinking symptoms. The usual term for this admixture of opposing but co-present moods and ways of thinking is 'mixed affective state'. I have avoided using this term because, in normal clinical parlance, it is used

to denote a state where the depressive and manic symptoms are both pathological. The situation here is a little
different in that much, if not all, of the depressive features
are co-extensive with what one might expect to find in
the early stages of grief, particularly one altered by its
occurring in an abnormal personality. One can imagine,
for example, that some onlookers might say that Jean took
her mother's death well, or stoically, because of an absence
of tears, sadness or agitation. My contention would be that
part of the burden that people with personality disorders
must carry is that the benefits of having easily recognised
responses are not open to them, so they are a puzzle both
to themselves and to others.

Signed
Andrew Harold

FINAL NARRATIVE *of*
ANTHONY SPARROW

I read the report sitting, uncomfortably, on an upside-down packing case in the old man's library. Pulling off my balaclava, I skimmed the list of psychiatric symptoms present, careless of them, overwhelmed by pity, immense pity for the girl. Although few would countenance it, I understood her predicament, sympathised with it, better than many would, or ever could, and I will explain why.

Usually, I do not talk about my parents; actually, the stark truth is no one is interested enough to ask. Why should they be? I am a seventy-six-year old man, plump to obese, with white hair that looks as though I have recently been electrocuted. Locks like Albert Einstein's, I reassure myself, when by mistake I am startled by my own reflection in a shop window. If asked about myself, I would say that I resemble a caricature paedophile in a cheap, unimaginative TV drama. Channel 5, perhaps? Even in my own life, in which I star, I would be played by a character actor.

On the whole, people do not like me, or 'get' me. They never have. Had I siblings I suspect they might have recoiled too. I am what used to be described as an 'acquired taste', but so pungent (think anchovies stuffed with capers and coated in marmite) as to make the many gag. Did you guess?

But enough of this cogitation, this self-indulgent claptrap.

My father died when I was seven and, to be frank, I have less recollection of him than of our family dog at the time, Snuff. An unpleasant little snapper, unhealthily fond of the ladies and obsessed with his own nether regions. My mother is a different matter. Beautiful. I loved her with all my heart until the day she died. And beyond, to this very second, till my own heart ceases to beat. In my childhood, she was my protectress, my companion, my playmate. She translated the world for me, and me to the world. As you will have gathered, few have loved me but she did, and if such a commodity is rare, those that bestow it are all the more treasured in return.

On her fiftieth birthday, after blowing out the candles on a Victoria sponge iced with butter cream (made by me), she broke the news that she had been diagnosed with cancer of the ovaries. My world collapsed. Three little words that express, for me, the truth, the end of everything. The darkening of my sun, moon and stars and the first day of my perpetual winter. Somehow, I tended her to her end, doing my daily tasks whilst witnessing her suffering, watching her bone-white arms and legs become sticks and her beloved head a skull. A curl of her lovely auburn locks lives in a locket by my bed. Morphine was supplied but not enough, and the sounds of her screams haunt me yet. They are the music of my nightmares. Two days before she died, blue veins now visible through translucent skin, she asked me to 'hurry' her on her journey. Obviously, I knew what she meant, but I pretended not to. Twice more, she begged me. Looked me in the eyes and entreated me with her whole being to release her. To my eternal shame, cowardice held me back, the thought that I might be caught and sent to prison. Normal people do not fare well in such institutions, the fate of abnormal ones (like me) does not bear thinking about. I look like a 'Beastie', remember. So, as you will by now have gathered, I failed her. Jean had passed the test that I failed. Filled with love for her great-uncle (and how distant is that, for pity's sake!) she was prepared to 'hurry' him on his journey, take the consequences, too. To do that had taken extraordinary courage. It was not a sign of madness, whatever any long-winded shrink might opine. Not in my book anyway.

Tears running down my blotchy cheeks, crying for me, for my darling mother as much as the girl, I tried to distract myself by leafing through the Family Book now balanced on my corduroyed knee. I had no doubt that this was the possession that she wished to obtain. It is a magnificent volume (bound in full tree calf with raised boards and rich gilt decoration to the spine, including a red label), and whilst it caters to a minority interest I have no doubt that it has some substantial monetary value, being both a work of considerable scholarship and a form of black exhibit, absolutely unique in its way. And, of course, its provenance is impeccable. Jean could not be expected to know it, but it is, in fact, a most marketable tome. Regardless of its marketability, I was now determined to return it to its true owner as soon as possible. I recognised her heroism and would do anything I could to see it was rewarded.

Struck with the thought of how bleak it all was, I saw that the pedigree of the Anstruthers of Strathdonald ended abruptly, and incompletely, with Allan Archibald, father of Isabel and Alexander. For them, there was, simply, a blank, a sea of white paper waiting to be filled in. It looked like an amputation. The Anstruther tree, you might say, had been pollarded and she, I felt sure, intended it to blossom once more in ink at least, and maybe later, in blood. While I was pondering on this fact, touched by it, my phone went and I could see from the display that my caller was Letitia Swinburne, a body I encourage to monitor the Obituaries (*Times* and *Telegraph*) for me. The widow of a Bart, on commission only, but with an address book Ashmole himself would have envied. If I acted *immediatement*, she whispered through a mouth clogged with baked meats, I might be able to offer to 'clear' a three-storey house in Berwick-on-Tweed, belonging to a someone called Lord Bartlett. My contact, whilst relishing her canapes at the wake had, in accordance with my usual instructions, already made the appropriate preliminary overtures on my behalf. In fact, the likely executor had my card, at this moment, in the pocket of his black Crombie. The name Bartlett immediately rang a bell. While I was still pulling myself together, damp hankie in hand, I noticed a copy of an up-to-date Burke's *Peerage, Baronetage and Knightage* on one of Anstruther's shelves. It seemed a Godsend. Dropping the hankie, desperate to look Bartlett up, convinced I had come across his name before and hoping against hope that it was, as I suspected, as a member of the Roxburghe Club, I rose hurriedly and removed the volume from the bookcase. As I opened it, a piece of thin, semi-translucent paper floated out from between the frontispiece and the guard sheet, landing on the floor at my feet.

I reproduce its contents below.

    – No 653 (FAMILY)

    – 1st March 2014

    – Isabel Euphemia Anstruther

    – DOB: 17th January 1941

    – Primary and Secondary Education:
St George's School, Edinburgh

    – Tertiary Education: Graduate of Edinburgh
College of Art (Paterson Travelling Scholarship)

    – (Had child (Camilla) 15th November 1962 (child adopted (McIntyre) – Edinburgh Sheriff Court – 29th December 1962) Decide whether to include? – see below)

    – Teacher (Painting): Edinburgh College of Art

    – Exhibitions:

            – Dundas Street Gallery, Edinburgh

            – Royal Dublin Art Society, Dublin

            – Marshalsea Gallery, Edinburgh

            – The Art Club, Aberdeen.

    – Hobbies/Interests: Natural History,
Australian Aboriginal Art.

    – DOD: 23rd September 1979. Died as a result of an accident on the Perth to Dundee Road.

Having checked on Bartlett and found that my memory had not been playing tricks upon me (indeed a club member since 1999), I phoned Letitia and instructed her in the appropriate technique for playing this particular salmonid and landing it, before leaving it to the tender mercies of my priest. Then, and only then, did I turn my attention back to the thin sheet.

I am, as you may have deduced, no fool. On the tracing paper was Alexander Anstruther's working for at least one new entry into the family tree. The scribbles provided, amongst other things, the details of Camilla's birth, the location of the Adoption Court, adoption date and adoption name. That Jean, too, had seen the document was vouchsafed by her writing on it the catalogue number and the description of the type of document as 'Family'. How astonishing, I mused, how moving, that her fingers had felt that piece of paper, one that unbeknownst to her included such information about her own blood: her mother and her grandmother.

Suddenly, I longed to see Jean, speak to her. I wanted to let her know that I, if no one else, understood, truly understood.

On impulse, I took my phone from my trouser pocket and contacted Saughton there and then. All that I could be told, a rough male voice informed me, was that Ms Whitadder had been discharged and was now living in a flat in the city. Ringing the Probation Service next, morphing myself into cousin Chris visiting from Tassie (to evade Data Protection once more), I obtained the exact address from the God-be-praised Australian officer. Of course I would keep it to myself, I reassured her, adding, as I felt sounded appropriate, 'it's the least I can do after your kindness'. We talked about the sights I should see: the Castle, the National Galleries and, of course, Greyfriars Bobby. Oh, the little dog? I asked. The little dog, she confirmed. Things having gone so well, I then over-reached myself trying for Jean's mobile number. At such a bold request, Beverley retreated like a hermit crab into its shell, murmuring something or other about 'job's worth'.

'If you're ever in Hobart . . .' I said weakly, but I knew I had lost her.

I put the book, first, into a large, padded envelope and then into an orange Sainsburys carrier bag and drove to the address in Gorgie. It proved to be a plain sandstone Edwardian tenement, and I parked in a bay opposite its shiny, gloss-painted front door. The array of grimy, sello-taped names below the bell-pulls included no Whitadder, but I tried, several times and to no avail, the one marked 'J. Anstruther'. I would wait no more than an hour, I had determined, although there was no particular logic to my self-imposed timescale. If that did not work I intended to drop a note of my telephone number through the door and await her call.

So, again I sat alone in the Polo. Cold, time dragging, watching the pedestrians, speculating on their jobs, wondering why no one held anybody's hand anymore, how a woman on a mobility scooter could drive so fast without mowing the elderly down, and trying to work out which charity was employing the hoodie pair rattling their cans menacingly in the faces of tired commuters. A nun fled in terror from them, looking backwards before tangling herself in the lead of a guide dog and spiralling to the ground. Henceforth, on principle, MENCAP would get nothing from me.

As I was massaging my knee, trying to prevent my right leg from going to sleep, a lady came walking down the pavement. The woman was stylish, held her head high and seemed to emanate a grace, a cool authority. Released unexpectedly from behind a cloud, the sun caught her dark lustrous hair, illuminated her high cheekbones. Though her features seemed finer, her nose a little longer, I had no difficulty in recognising Jean Anstruther from our first meeting. I watched as a man she passed turned slyly around to get a second glance, and I understood his impulse. Maybe, when I saw her in Saughton, my perception of her had been coloured by her drab, grey surroundings, whereas here I was seeing her as she truly was, free, and, I have to use the word, beautiful. What her appeal was, precisely, I shall never know, but what I do know is that I did not wish to take my eyes off her. Maybe the thought of her remarkable selfless act coloured my judgement, clouded my judgement. All I can say is simply looking at her gave me unexpected pleasure, made me feel protective towards her as if she was some exquisite little plant that others might not appreciate and stamp upon. Standing directly in front of me, for a few seconds she bent her comely head to look in her shoulder bag for her key and then, as I knew she would, she opened the door of the tenement. I longed to follow her and lay my treasure at her feet.

Heart thudding, I took the Family Book out of its bag to admire it one last time. It fell open at the final page, bright sunshine pouring through the windscreen and illuminating it, and something caught my eye. On the back pastedown was the faintest pencil inscription in familiar, quavery capitals. All it said was

'CF
DOB 15th November 1962.
DOD 16th July 1965.'

'DOD'. I knew what it meant. Date of Death.

I put the book back in its bag, turned the key in the ignition and drove home.

Below I append a copy of Camilla Faulkner's death certificate.

B 55715

EXTRACT OF AN ENTRY IN A REGISTER OF DEATHS

kept under the Registration of Births, Deaths and Marriages (Scotland) Act 1960

District No. 685-5	Year 1965	Entry No. 143099

DEATH registered in the District of .... GEORGE SQUARE ....

in the .... CITY .... of .... EDINBURGH ....

(1) Name(s) and Surname	Camilla Alexandra Faulkner	(2) Sex F
(3) Occupation	N/A	
(4) Marital Status	single	(5) Date of Birth 15/ 11 / 1962 (6) Age 2
(7) Name, Surname and Occupation of Spouse(s)	——— ———	
(8) When and Where Died	Royal Infirmary, Edinburgh 16th July 1965	
(9) Usual Residence (if different from place of death)	34 Gloucester Circus, Edinburgh	

(10) Name(s), Surname and Occupation of Father	(11) Name(s), Surname(s) and Maiden Surname of Mother
Arthur James McIntyre - Archivist	Judith Elisabeth McIntyre nee Guild

(12) Cause of Death	I (a) — Peritonitis
	(b) — Ruptured appendix
	(c) —
Name and Qualifications of Medical Practitioner	II Dr Pauline Lowe

(13) Informant's Signature and Qualification	(Signed) Arthur McIntyre Father

| (14) Registrar's Signature | (Signed) |

Back in my own small, warm sitting-room I sat with my head in my hands, desolate, trying to work out exactly what had happened. A cup of tea rested, undrunk and tepid, on the arm of my chair. My first thought was that the woman had fooled her elderly, demented employer into believing that she was Camilla's daughter, his niece's offspring. That would explain the will so largely in her favour.

By the evening, now fuelled by cheap amontillado and too many twiglets, I came to reject that conclusion. Through his journal, possessions and house, I believed I had got to know Anstruther's character a little. He loved genealogy, revelled in his own, and valued accuracy. He was a man of science. In his writings he stated, time after time, that he was the End of the Line. Blood mattered to him above all. Only by the time he had forgotten his own name would he have forgotten his niece's demise. The capitals were in his distinctive writing.

Now, I am convinced that Ms Whitadder attempted to gull the old man, took considerable pains to do so, but that all her attempts failed. Faced with failure, I think, she murdered her employer and forged a new will. Forgery was a skill she possessed and amongst his papers was a copy of the original will and an accompanying solicitor's letter. I saw it myself later. All she had to do was use it like a legal style, alter it in her favour, reproduce the witnesses' signatures, and the less greedy she was the less likelihood of it being challenged. A share of only five-eighths did not elicit suspicion, in fact was judged perfectly. Not unreasonably, she expected, given her victim's advanced age and frail condition, to get away with it. Why should she not? Old men do die of old age and the vast majority do not undergo the indignity of a post mortem. Questions are not asked. Accelerating his death must have seemed like a small, fairly insignificant risk. Her only miscalculation was not to remove, or destroy, the Bad Blood Brigade letter. Because it was that which triggered the PM examination.

I admit it, I admire her cunning and her steely nerve. She went for broke. Accused of the smothering, she, originally, put forward a Not Guilty plea. A not unreasonable course given the old man's age and her Counsel's explanation about the difficulty for the Crown of proving, firstly, the smothering and, secondly, that she did it. If, for any reason, that appeared to be failing, she had a standby to rely on.

And she did. When the trial, from her perspective, began to take an unexpected direction (with Dr Willow's spectacularly inept performance) she cashed in her chips. At the back of her mind, I feel confident in asserting, she always had the possibility of relying on a 'mercy killing', should the need arise. All the work she had undertaken to convince the Professor of their cosanguinity, could be used to that end. Only those she now had to convince of her blood relationship were much less savvy, much less knowledgeable than him. If her own Counsel believed her, so, too, might her Prosecutor. And, oddly, what might have seemed like unparalleled good fortune for a mere employee, her legacy, could be used to fortify her assertion of a blood relationship. What had she to lose?

Thinking about it afresh, I suspect even her shrink fell for her. Consider his epilogue:

'My contention would be that part of the burden that people with personality disorders must carry is that the benefits of having easily recognised responses are not open to them, so they are a puzzle both to themselves and to others.'

His illustration of that 'burden' was that no one would recognise her genuine grief on the death of her mother. Now, if that was not included to evoke the Judge's sympathy for the woman, I'm a caterpillar. The likes of Garry, of course, would be putty in such an operator's hands, and I suspect he was either her dupe or, more likely, her devoted creature.

Injustice may pile upon injustice. Given the view the Court took of her supposedly compassionate action, is it possible that she will yet be able to inherit a significant portion of the Professor's estate once it has been ingathered? I phoned a lawyer acquaintance of mine, eager to please me as his whole being is crying out for my copy of Cowell's *Institutione Juris Anglicani*, and his advice was that it is a matter of the Court's discretion in such circumstances. And why should the court not exercise it in her favour? After all, they believe that this attractive young lady risked her own liberty to ease a dying man out of a life he no longer wished to live. A final act of love, God help us all.

But how, precisely, did she do it? Having done some surprisingly shallow burrowing, I now know that all she required to execute her plan was Camilla's adopted name, the date of the adoption and the name of the court that dealt with the adoption. If she had that information plus authority, in writing, by the adopted person, then she would be allowed to inspect the relevant adoption record. Someone like her would, of course, not baulk at a little more forgery. Document number 653 gave her all the information she required to fool the Records Office. The booty retrieved from Records, plus a little basic internet research, gave her everything she needed to become an imposter.

But is her mother alive? Was her own mother, in fact, adopted?

Her mother is dead, and, as I expected, died on the date she gives in her jottings. I checked this out subsequently, too. It is also true that her mother was adopted. The catalyst for the whole plan, I surmise, was the double oddity that her mother and Camilla had been adopted and, possibly, the more unusual fact that they shared a birthday. An additional piece of luck, if you can call it that, was the death of her mother. Assuming that she, too, was not of a criminal disposition, would she have gone along with such a scheme? Does bad blood exist? I cannot say for sure, but I doubt it. Mrs Whitadder was, indeed, the librarian at the Blackhall library, worked in the same building for twenty years and was well-respected by those of her colleagues that I managed to trace. 'The nicest of women', one said. Another described her as 'a real sweetie'. But her only child had her cremated with almost indecent haste.

The most convincing liars only fabricate what they need; buttress the structure created by their lies with easily ascertainable truths. Storytelling, in short.

Jean Whitadder's journal, of course, is a masterpiece of Creative Writing. That she had some sort of diary, I do not doubt, nor that she used it to produce this mixture of reality and fantasy. But I am satisfied that the document I copied for you was not concocted for any eyes other than my own. Why, you may wonder?

Because I had possession of the Family Book and had to be persuaded to return it to her. I had become involved in her life, another bit-part player to be enchanted by her, charmed by her, beguiled, used by her to get what she wanted. And then discarded. But she, like so many others, underestimated me. You see, I alone understand the true importance of that book.

CF is Camilla (Faulkner) McIntyre who died aged three. The date of her death is 16th July 1965. Of course, she had no child herself. I imagine that Jean Whitadder did not know what this scribble meant (or had not noticed it) when she first started on her plan, and only discovered it, or understood it, after it had failed.

Now, that particular scribble in the Family Book has acquired an additional meaning. It means Miss Whitadder's destruction. It reveals that she is a murderer, plain and simple. In many ways, I castigate myself for not realising that something was amiss sooner than I did. Her writings may be the outpourings of a devious, dishonest mind, but the only unreliability in the Professor's account stems, I would hazard, from his great age, general health (particularly his progressing Alzheimer's disease) and his increasingly close proximity to the most talented of liars. I repeat, he told us, time after time, that he was the end of the line.

As you now know, I have not passed the Family Book on to that woman. It rests securely on my own shelves, rubbing spines with other beautifully bound, finely tooled volumes. It is a prize in itself. In case you should wonder, I have still not been in touch with the police. A Moriarty requires a Holmes, not a plodder, a flatfoot. Anyway, they had their chance and blew it. No, I am content simply to publish this slim volume, let it find its way into the world and enlighten it. Thus do I betray her trust. By now, for aught known, that sophisticated tale-spinner may be on her way to becoming a lawyer, perhaps a bewigged Sheriff ready to test 'the credibility and reliability' of those in the dock. Takes one to know one? Nothing would surprise me about the hopes and dreams of that cunning little colleen. Would the Law Society contemplate such a thing? Why not, she will have 'paid her dues' to society, and 'change' and redemption are all the rage.

I, as I admitted to you, am little more than a humble bookworm and burying beetle, but in my years upon the earth I have learnt a few handy things about the Law. To wit, I know that I must collect my debts within five years otherwise they will have been extinguished simply by the passage of time. I know that no one can own something stolen even if they have paid for it. I got my fingers burnt with that one before (Quesnay's *Traité de la Gangrene* nearly cost me my whole hand) and, I suppose, my present custody of the

Family Book (if it was, indeed, gifted, *inter vivos*?) may be on the tenuous side.

Perhaps, the putative remaining member of the Anstruther family may attempt to acquire it from me? I would, of course, have to be satisfied as to the validity of any claim and, in any event, it is worth its weight in gold to me. Sentiment, on the part of the seller (never mind the purchaser), always adds value. On reflection, perhaps, for the right price I could overlook any problems in title? For safety, I will deposit it in the bank, as there may be rapacious people abroad, some of them may even know my address. There is one other gobbet of law that I've digested, but which, to be frank, I never thought I would need. On the other hand, none of us know what (or who) is around the corner in life, do we? It is this.

A defence to an action of libel is Veritas. The truth, if you please. So, be prepared, Miss Whitadder, should you ever have the temerity to resort to law, I am ready and waiting for you. Oh yes, one other thing. Remember those hairbrushes I passed on to the grateful 'Rough' Andrea? Luckily, I did not pass on the matching silver and ivory comb, the third part of the set. I still have it. Woven between the yellowed teeth are strands of white hair, waiting to be harvested by me. It is currently in the bank. Should you find some ingenious way around the death certificate, I understand DNA can resolve everything about parentage nowadays. I told you more than once, Missy, I am no fool.

Anthony Sparrow